FLAME IN A HIGH WIND

Jacqueline Kidd

It's 1814 and years of war are in Captain Denny Poynter's blood and there is no way to stop killing now that peace is at hand. They call him a common pirate and both the British and the Americans hunt him relentlessly. But only with the beautiful Renee is he a helpless captive . . .

FLAME IN A HIGH WIND

Jacqueline Kidd

Curley Publishing, Inc.
South Yarmouth, Ma.

Library of Congress Cataloging-in-Publication Data

Kidd, Jacqueline.
  Flame in a high wind / Jacqueline Kidd.
    p. cm.
  1. Large type books. I. Title.
  [PS3561.I328F55   1990]
  813'.54—dc20
  ISBN 0–7927–0543–2 (lg. print)   90–35794
  ISBN 0–7927–0544–0 (pbk.: lg. print)   CIP

Published in Large Print by arrangement with Dorchester Publishing, Inc. in the United States, Canada, the U.K. and British Commonwealth and the rest of the world market.

Distributed in Great Britain, Ireland and the Commonwealth by CHIVERS LIBRARY SERVICES LIMITED, Bath BA1 3HB, England.

Printed in Great Britain

FLAME IN A HIGH WIND

ONE

From an easterly point on the Connecticut shore, given a clear day, a good telescope and a seaman's vision, it was possible to stand and obtain a good view of his country's humiliation – or at least a convincing part of the cause: the blockading vessels of the British navy. They cruised at will along the length and breadth of Long Island Sound, maintaining the throttling grip which was gradually strangling the United States on its own doorstep.

Bransom Hubbard had had two looks in as many days, making the trip out from the protected inland waters, going once by sloop, again by horse, viewing anew every current and landmark, studying the ships as they showed off the point. He'd seen a big frigate, a seventy-four, even reading the name on her bows – *Indefatigable*. All unsuspecting, her captain had come briefly into his view, standing with legs widespread on his quarter-deck, square-built and heavy set as the British bulldog – this by contrast with Hubbard's Yankee leanness and height. Like his ship, the Englishman would be a

1

worthy antagonist, should they chance to meet somewhere in those waters, as was entirely possible within the next few days or even hours.

Like a shadow to the frigate had been a smaller, sleeker craft, built along the lines of the American privateers – aptly named *Racer*. Either ship might prove a mean antagonist. As a pair they would be formidable.

Rain slapped Hubbard's face, solid as the wind behind it. Blobs of snow intermingled wetly. By nightfall these would be sleet. A perfect night for remaining snug before a roaring fire. But the more impossible the weather from a sailor's standpoint, the better for that of man and ships to break the blockade.

Tonight would be the night.

Hubbard checked his swinging stride, staring, instinctively drawing his oilskins closer at the neck. Off there, tugging to the conflicting swell of river and tide, as impatient with her anchor as a blooded horse, was the *Lively Lady* – scheduled, almost as certainly as the *Red Savage*, to make the attempt at freedom. Twin ships of the same shipyard, alike from the laying of their keels, hustled furiously to completion by rival crews, driven by a not always friendly animosity.

The *Lively Lady!* A perfect name for such

2

a ship, particularly when so christened by her captain and certainly with a most special lady in mind. The Lady Renee d'Ernee – gay, laughing Renee, exiled all her days, unquenchable as a flame even in a high wind –

Denny Poynter, as her captain, had had the naming of her. Hubbard gave grudging approval for the choice. On that point at least they thought alike.

But the *Lively Lady* was altered since he'd last seen her, some days before. Subtly, yet so unmistakably as to affect even her character. Hubbard sucked in a deep breath, his head-shake angry. It was clear enough now. A life-sized figure perched at her bows, leaning far out, eagerly, fearlessly, as though to lead the way; the Lively Lady herself – and again, however blurred by the storm, a perfect match and representation of the figurehead which adorned the *Red Savage*.

That wooden hulk transfigured almost to a living thing beneath chisel and knife, carved with loving remembrance by himself over the entire period when the *Savage* had been a-building. Afterward, when carefully painted and finally affixed in place, Hubbard had known a more than creative satisfaction. Not only would the Lady lead them through turmoil and adventure to victory, but she

3

rendered the *Red Savage* distinctive, above and apart from Poynter's vessel.

Not to be outdone, Poynter had somehow managed a duplicate, undoubtedly setting several skilled artisans to the task, taking turns, working around the clock. Again, outwardly, there was nothing but their names to distinguish the pair of privateers.

Hubbard shrugged, continuing on. Whatever honor there was, Renee deserved it.

At mid-afternoon, the blow gave every evidence of turning into a full-blown Nor'easter – the sort of storm for which Captain Henderson – Mad Josh – himself and the crew of the *Red Savage* had been hoping, almost praying, since she had been completed and provisioned.

On ahead he glimpsed the *Red Savage*, also straining at her anchor, nearly shut away by the increasing beat of storm. He envisioned what was in store for them. At his feet stretched the Connecticut shore, the inland waters protected by Forts Schuyler and Totten, with Montauk Point and Block Island ghostly and lost on such a day. As river merged to sound there were treacherous narrows to be coursed on their way out, waters dangerous even under favoring conditions, doubly so with ships of war lying in wait.

4

Back in here, protected by the forts, hammers rang defiantly to the stutter of saws as ships sprang to being like the fruit of a scatter of dragon's teeth. The sulphurous breath of Sharkey Poynter's shipyards battled the snow.

For the matter of that, he was still breathing fire.

The figurehead proved anew that Denny Poynter, like himself, continued to think of Renee, to remember.

This coming voyage of the *Lively Lady* would be Denny Poynter's first essay against the enemy. For himself, Hubbard had been out twice, initially as a third officer, then as the second, and because of the record he'd compiled, he was going now as first mate aboard the *Savage*, picked by Mad Josh Henderson from among a score of applicants. To sail with Mad Josh was in itself an accolade. Still short of middle age, he was the Old Man of the Sea in person, and if there was a touch of wildness to the man and his methods, it was tempered by genius. Mad Josh had learned his business under Decatur.

Increasingly, the blockade imposed along the American coasts grew more strangling. Slowly, inexorably, pressure and hardships were taking their toll of the nation. And with the news filtering across from the

5

Continent, it became increasingly vital that more ships should break out from protected harbors, to retaliate. Wellington was gathering his strength, Wellington was on the move. Napoleon, staggered before Moscow, had never full recouped his former prestige or strength. Wellington was set for a final, knockout blow.

If and when that came, England, freed after two decades of a war for survival against the relentless Corsican, would be able to turn its full strength against America, to increase the pressure. These twin privateers must win free and hit hard, to somewhat even the contest.

Two vessels, fashioned for speed and striking power, built in the same shipyards, yet rivals from the laying of their keels. Which would suit old Sharkey Poynter perfectly. Rivalry between captains and crews enhanced the worth of ships.

Father and son did not necessarily see alike. Denny Poynter had scarcely been able to conceal his outrage when he had learned that Bran Hubbard would be second in command of the *Red Savage*.

That the two ships should essay the adventure of running the gauntlet together was somehow fitting and proper, even as it was ironical that delays and weather had timed it so for both. It might even be that they could

6

assist each other against the common enemy, partly by dividing the watchfulness of the blockaders, or at need by fighting together. In alliance, they could prove formidable.

Renee, with hair like dawn mist, a slip of a maid, lovely as a dream. Hubbard remembered a dainty foot apeep from beneath a sweep of skirts, topped by that flashing smile and the hale of hair which even then could set hearts aflame. And the fingers of boys, of men, at each others' throats.

Renee! Aristocratic to the tilt of saucy nose and tip of pointed shoes, as became the daughter of a Marquis of France, yet as surely democratic in her instincts as those who had overthrown the order to which her father clung, as though born instead in the States, rather than transplanted awhile to be neighbor to Bran Hubbard, friend and playmate and laughing comrade.

Not quite neighbor or playfellow to the son of the shipyard's owner, though, once he had set eyes upon her, Denny Poynter had insisted on intruding whenever and wherever possible. Even Renee's coolness, her frequent rebuffs, the occasional chastisement of Hubbard's fists, had not discouraged him.

Hubbard could not entirely blame him. If Poynter cared half so much for her as he did, nothing would ever stop him from striving to win her. Like Helen of Troy, she was that sort of a woman. Or as the old sachem of the Oneidas had once put it, what man, having seen the sun, would be content with the moon?

Renee! Now, of course, grown to womanhood, and long gone from the Connecticut shore, but leaving behind a memory fresh and breathless as the springtime – along with other and harsher recollections, such as the bloody noses when he and Denny Poynter had clashed for her favor. Poynter had been furious that from the first she had bestowed it upon Bran Hubbard, for all that his father was merely a dock worker instead of owner of a great shipyard, and he awkward and gangly by comparison with the graceful poise and good looks of Denny.

However rebuffed, Poynter had remained persistent, openly boasting, when Renee and her parents and brother had said good-by to their American sanctuary and set sail for England, that one day he would follow and find her for himself, carrying her off if need be. It had sounded gallant, even swashbuckling, but Renee, blinking back tears, had turned to Hubbard, leaving heart-break in her wake.

In those days Bran had not understood very well the twists of international politics, forces which had caused their removal to England. It had seemed strange, since France and England were at war; the illogic was that the Marquis d'Ernee supported the deposed Bourbons against the upstart Corsican.

England, as the world had seemed to children who throughout their lives had known nothing else, had been always at war with Napoleon and France, but not then with America.

Hubbard blinked unseeingly against the storm. There had been the time when he'd kissed Renee; the one when Poynter had come upon them, murderously –

On that day of parting he had managed a word with her, even if not alone; where she had broken-heartedly reciprocated his confession of undying love.

Now her likeness, on the one hand carved painstakingly by his own hands, adorned both ships. If the years had brought no change in his own feelings, apparently Denny Poynter remained unchanged as well. But it was increasingly likely that, grown to womanhood, Renee might forget; that she would continue to care was as unlikely as that they would ever meet again.

TWO

Poynter had come up unobserved. Nothing was changed. "I suppose Mad Josh is thinking of making a break for it tonight," Denny taunted. "If you're a smart enough set of seamen, maybe you can follow the *Lively Lady*. That's the only way you'd ever manage."

"There's a difference between wind in the sails and wind in the mouth," Hubbard retorted, and for a moment thought that the old battle would be renewed. But it was confirmation that, like Mad Josh, Poynter was determined on the attempt.

His derision left Hubbard untroubled. Across the years he and his seamanship had been tried, harshly and repeatedly. It was not because of favoritism that he had been picked by Mad Josh for second in command, when lines of other men, experienced and eager, had begged for such a chance. This would be his third venture aboard a privateer.

Both voyages had been brief, but on the first he had brought back a sinking ship, assuming command when both her captain and first and second officers had died in the fierceness of battle; brought her in through the blockade to beach her, loaded with commodities doubly precious to the country, saving her crew from capture or drowning.

On the second try he'd been put aboard a prize vessel, also richly laden, and had brought her in through a hail of shells.

He could barely make out the *Red Savage* as he came upon her, swaying uneasily to her anchor, with rigging groaning protest to the lash of wind. Flurries had given place to driving snow. On such a night, most ships would stand well away from shore, or huddle snug in anchorage. Mad Josh waited with a savage patience, not even pacing. Hubbard was well to the time set.

"A bit of a blow," Mad Josh greeted with typical understatement. " 'Tis what we've waited for. At your convenience, Mr. Hubbard, we'll have the anchor up, then try a run at it."

Hubbard gave necessary orders. The snow was taking form, blurring outlines, lending its visibility in what otherwise would have been total blackness. A rounded mound had heaped around the square base of the binnacle. The long slope of the deck, heeling to the drag of wind and tide against the anchor, showed white.

Mad Josh assumed charge as they began

11

to move, voicing orders in a restrained tone, as though apprehensive that they might somehow be overheard by his rival captain half a mile away, or even aboard the ships of the British, forced to unenviable patrol. Then, facing into the wind and making no effort to shelter from the drive of snow, Mad Josh left the actual operation of the *Red Savage* to Hubbard, while keeping a sharpened attention for every move.

Men, long cooped ashore, scrambled eagerly aloft, contemptuous alike of the enemy and the numbing cold. Everyone aboard was trained, unlike the scourings to which the years of war had reduced the British. They clung as much by instinct as agility to the icy ratlines, setting the fore and main topmast staysails, reefing, sheeting them home. Even in the protected waters of the sound the *Red Savage* leaped like a hungry trout.

Frozen canvas crackled as it unrolled. Ropes snapped like pistol shots, a storm of ice rained down. Eyes strained for vanished landmarks. These first hours and miles would be dangerous, as treacherous from wild waters and hidden banks as from the lurking enemy.

Once out, Mad Josh would run with all the sail the *Red Savage* could sustain, her master reckless always to the point of near-disaster.

12

Nothing less could enable them to win the wild battle for escape.

The river had been left behind, and they were into the widening channel. Hubbard could tell by the increasing leap and plunge, the *Savage* lying far over to the wind. Sight was a matter of instinct, even guesswork; a mistake of either could be disastrous. But with Mad Josh giving an occasional order, his own knowledge of these dark waters matching, they were taking her out. A little more, and they would cross to the open sea, and from there their chances would be as good as those of any other vessel on such a night.

Mad Josh was studying the compass in the light of the binnacle, sharpening his calculations. Hubbard stirred, aware that he was plastered with snow, conscious for the first time of the numbing bite of cold. Like Henderson, he had been too intent on each crowding moment, with instant decision and calls for action, to give heed to the weather as it affected himself. Now he stamped his feet and swung his arms. Two hours – three. In the night he had lost count of time.

Members of the crew huddled in such shelter as they could find, ready for action. With a guilty start Hubbard remembered and relieved the man at the wheel.

They were out – or almost. Triumph surged

13

in wild elation. Denny Poynter had sent a messenger during the afternoon with added word for Hubbard.

"Your *Savage* will never match my *Lively Lady* – just as you will never match me with the Lady herself!"

At least, Poynter did not lack for egotism. In one aspect Hubbard believed him. Somewhere the three of them would meet again. It was as surely fated as the stars in their courses.

Eyes straining, he glimpsed a speck over the starboard, whiter than the gray drive of snow. Almost automatically he leaped and climbed, feeling a fresh rush of sympathy for the crew, forced aloft under such conditions. The rigging had re-iced, spidery as a web. Above the deck the gale shrieked with redoubled fury, while the sea hissed far beneath. A loss of grip, a single misstep, could hurtle a man to swift and certain death.

There it was again, that whiteness the spray from the plunging bows of a ship. Now the lookout had seen and was bawling a warning. Mad Josh was there as Hubbard regained the deck. A ship, close-hauled like themselves under storm canvas. Now it was almost abreast, and he caught the curved bow, the broad strips of paint, with a double checkered line, sure identification. She was

14

a two-decker, a Britisher. In the night and storm they had all but smashed into each other.

He wondered if she might be the *Indefatigable*. Somehow, as between Poynter and himself, between these ships he had a feeling of inevitability, as though storm and tide drove them toward a common destiny.

THREE

That had been close, a game, not of bluff but of blind men in the night, both vessels taking risks which at other times would be accounted madness. Each was lost almost as swiftly as they had come upon one another, and anxious straining of eyes showed nothing more.

All things wear out, even endless night. Hubbard forced himself to increased alertness with the approach of dawn. Out here the seas were no less stormy, but with a savagery more controlled. It was unlikely that the paths of the two ships might cross again or so soon, but it was in being prepared for the unusual and the unexpected that a good captain kept a ship under him.

The lookout saw it first, bawling a hoarse

15

warning. Neither Mad Josh nor Hubbard had set foot below decks, maintaining a half-frozen vigil through that decisive night. It would tell the tale, whether they were free to rove as they would, or should be trapped at the outset.

Hubbard had set men to shoveling away the snow. It coated everything with an icy sharpness. This was bitter weather even for New Englanders, for Yankees accustomed to the vagaries of the eastern seaboard. He swung at the hail. As the *Savage* ascended a wave, heaving out of a tumble of water, he glimpsed the patch far astern, a square of white no bigger than a lady's handkerchief.

It was gone again, the *Savage* plunging down the slope. Mad Josh muttering what both had recognized – the fore-topsail not merely of a ship, but almost certainly of the Britisher whom they had glimpsed at such close range during the night. Chance or the luck of an able master, guessing the course they must follow, had kept them fairly close throughout the night.

Presently it showed again, somewhat closer; a two-decker, a tub in a moderate sea, from which the *Red Savage* could walk away almost as though the other ship were anchored. But in winds and seas such as these the advantage lay with the heavier vessel. The *Red Savage*

16

was plunging madly to the canvas which Mad Josh had crowded on, her grace and litheness gone in a savage progress from wave to wave. Leaning far over, she was doubly in danger of disaster, prey to the elements.

The two-decker was gaining. No doubt now, she was a frigate, carrying twice the armament of the privateer, her scantlings perhaps twice as thick. The lighter guns of the *Savage* would have trouble in piercing her defences except at point-blank range. And in these furious waters, the very clumsiness of her weight and bulk lent her a steadiness for working the guns which the madly plunging *Savage* could no longer do.

If only the wind would abate, even by a very little! Not much would be required to even the speed and sailing qualities between them. And then, as though a fervent if unvoiced prayer had been answered, the wind dropped somewhat, veering a point or so.

The improvement was marked if not complete. The *Red Savage* regained a measure of that dancing eagerness which everyone aboard had been certain she would show. There was a reasonable chance now that they could hold their distance, then, with improving conditions, run away from the big frigate, beginning to lumber in her turn.

But luck was always qualitative. A second

patch of white showed, coming at them from an angle, gaining. Again Hubbard and Mad Josh exchanged glances, and neither needed to voice what they knew. It was another Britisher – smaller, faster in normal seas than the frigate, less heavily armed. But in concert they could be deadly.

Mad Josh was never a man to hesitate nor slow to make up his mind. He gave prompt orders for a change in course, and the crew, understanding, set up a hoarse shout. Dangerous as it was, the move met with their approval. He was swinging the *Savage* to dart between the closing ships, rather than continuing impossible retreat. If the maneuver worked, and it was clearly catching them by surprise, they would be very close as she swept between –

Mad Josh was proposing to fight, and even a single, smaller ship, well-handled, would have a fighting chance. Mistimed by even a fraction, she would be a sitting duck amid birds of prey, to be raked by successive broadsides from each, crippled or put out of action before she could even hope to retaliate. Against the two, she would be heavily outgunned and outmanned.

But there would come a certain point, an instant when neither of the foes would dare fire for the risk of hitting each other, and a

18

captain who knew his business could respond with deadly effect, loosing broadsides at each almost simultaneously. The gun crews of the *Savage* were standing ready and eager, and the *Savage*, responding ever more nimbly as the seas grew more to her liking, made a lively target as she darted to the climax.

As his attention focused on the impending duel, the lookout shouted, proclaiming yet another sail on the horizon. Mad Josh lost his normal taciturnity. He loosed an exultant whoop. "It's the *Lively Lady!* Between us we can make a kill!"

It was, indeed, the *Lively Lady*, bearing down fast, as though fearful of being left out from sharing a valuable capture. Hubbard reflected that his thought might be a little unworthy, however natural, knowing Poynter as he did. Her presence indeed could make a difference. While alone the best that the *Red Savage* might hope for was to partially cripple the smaller British vessel, perhaps doing some damage to the frigate, then, in the confusion, outsail them, the oncoming *Lady* shifted the weight of armament. If she continued to hold her present course, she might also pour a devastating hail at the smaller craft, so that between them they might put her out of action.

Faced with such a reversal, the frigate

19

could hardly do better than hope for a stalemate. Her guns would still outreach, but with lessening wind and wave they both could outsail her, darting about like terriers harassing a stag.

Now Hubbard had a glimpse of the two-decker's name, and not at all to his surprise, it was the *Indefatigable*.

Mad Josh was lost in a smother of spray. He lifted a hand, and Hubbard relayed the order, their broadside let loose – its roar smothered in a greater as *Indefatigable* chose that precise moment for her own. The range, while not point-blank, was too close for even indifferent gunners to do badly. Hubbard was aware of whistling noises in his ear, of a splintering crash as a mast was shattered and toppled, wreckage and splinters filling the air. At least one cannon ball from the seventy-four had scored a direct, damaging hit. Smoke enveloped them like fog.

Their own guns were responding, thrown off-target as the *Savage* heeled to the blow. Mad Josh was stretched, face down, unstirring. Hubbard's eyes took note, even as his mind refused to respond to the disaster. There was no time, not with a battle to be fought. The smaller vessel staggered to their blast, heeling, unable to respond until too late. He glimpsed her name, again without surprise. *Racer.*

A beginning roar of triumph from the crew subsided to a whisper, altering to an incredulous growl.

The *Lively Lady* had held on, approaching for a look, but now she swung sharply, strangely silent. Then she was scuttling away at a pretty clip, deserting them without firing a shot, while the two Britishers, swift to recover, closed for the kill.

FOUR

Hubbard remained cool, even while his mind burned at the calculated treachery. Again, having known Denny Poynter all his days, his reaction was understandable. It was not cowardice, though under the circumstances it came close to treason. Nor was it alone a lack of willingness to share a prize and a victory; rather it was a chance for the royal navy to rid him at the outset of this voyage of the enemy he had hated increasingly over the years.

That they might do so within the next few moments seemed more than a possibility. Confusion, the wild yawing of the *Red Savage*

21

as her steersman also had been stricken, had altered everything. Another man had the wheel, but sails cluttered the deck, debris and dead men were everywhere. She was in no position to run for it, there was no time to reload, win position, and make a fight of it. But with the savage push of the wind, she was moving again.

"Hold her steady!" It was the order Mad Josh would have given, a mad choice but the only possible one left to them. Hubbard braced for the impact as they drove straight at the onrushing *Indefatigable*. Almost certainly the collision would send them to the bottom, but with even a little luck, they'd take the bigger ship with them. They were ships of war, and the winning of a battle, not survival, was the object of such strife. It would be more a victory than defeat.

He heard the wild screech of a shouted order, trumpeted at the last possible moment, watched as the dark hulk of the two-decker surged past, so close that he might almost have reached to touch her, heard then the greater, splintering crash as, changing course with such abruptness, the frigate cut through her sister ship, clawing about to deliver a broadside of her own. The *Racer* was cut in half, overriden.

Mad Josh was reviving, coming unsteadily

to his feet, a red welt across his forehead; the hit of a flying piece of debris had been less serious than Hubbard had first feared. They were out, having run the blockade. With improving weather the ravages could soon be repaired. Only the memory of Poynter's desertion in the face of peril remained like a stink in the nostrils. With the rest of the crew having seen, there could be no room for doubt. To all save Hubbard, it was unbelievable.

"The gr-reat coward!" Mad Josh raved, once he heard the account. "Because we'd have shared the win, he prefers to allow them still to harass the seas – and ourselves, as he hoped, forced to run, while it's himself is the stinkin' traitor!"

The hunting proved fair to good as they roved, scuttling from the frigid north toward the warmer seas which washed the Indies, working gradually toward the Continent, toward England itself. If peril increased in such waters, so did the shipping upon which they might prey. That it was improved by Mad Josh's willingness, even eagerness, to take chances, was attested by the record. It was all in the log which Mad Josh kept meticulously. The number of encounters, of fights, some harsh and bitter, most of which they had turned to victories – though

23

forced a few times to retreat before superior numbers and fire-power. In all, the number of prizes taken, sent to friendly ports under prize crews, totaled rather high.

Having a practical Yankee turn of mind, Hubbard estimated the share which by now must be deposited to his account in various firms and banks. It was not a side of war which particularly interested him, the profits to be derived from the capture or destruction of ships of the enemy or of neutrals engaged in a profitable if risky commerce with that enemy. They, like he, were doing their best according to their sympathies and opportunities. To come to sudden ruin was no less bitter through actions of war than from the depredations of pirates.

Unquestionably he was profiting. By war's end, even if came tomorrow, he would rate a relatively rich man.

There were some unsatisfied even with such chances for profit; some, from increasing reports, who were turning to open privacy, an avid preying on the helpless wherever they might be found. As was apparently the case with Denny Poynter.

Hubbard at first had refused to believe. He'd never held a high opinion of Denny, still he was a neighbor, a fellow-American, and certainly in no need for any desperate seeking of riches. But reports persisted. The hunting of English ships had not been too good. There were those who insisted that he had turned to the hunting of almost any and all – but especially and worst, against the ships of his own people.

Greed knew no flag.

Even that was not the worst. The *Red Savage* and the *Lively Lady* had been built in the same shipyards to matching specifications, and the seas were wide. The reports which confirmed Poynter's infamy added the news that his ship sailed now as the *Red Savage*, that the outrages she was piling up were being attributed to them.

" 'Tis no matter for surprise," Mad Josh growled. "When he turned tail and ran he showed his colors – not as a coward, for he's no such. But for his real self."

At first Hubbard had refused to believe, but any remaining doubts were erased when from the deck of the *Red Savage* they sighted something which at a distance looked to be a life-boat. On closer approach, three men sprawled in its bottom, their pinched faces and contorted positions evidence of suffering and privation. Two were alive, though barely.

Hubbard superintended the transfer of the survivors to the rescue boat and thence to the deck of the *Savage*, then made sure that the life-boat was hoisted in turn. One of the pair succumbed almost as they brought him to the deck, but the third, painfully swallowing a dollop of grog and water, revived enough to talk – to curse the piratical, cutthroat crew of the *Lively Lady* and her captain, whom he had recognized from long-gone days along the Connecticut shore. He died as he spoke, as though his strength had lasted only to denounce that crew and its captain. Mad Josh listened, his eyes increasingly bright with the touch of madness.

Hubbard showed him the life-boat, even though no further confirmation was needed. Originally the name of its ship, the *Lively Lady*, had been lettered on its side. That had been painted over, the covering imperfect. Superimposed above that was the *Red Savage*.

The *Red Savage* was his ship, and in the eyes of Mad Josh, it was nothing less than blasphemy. He raised great fists to the sky.

"A devil's ship, and captained by a devil!" he pronounced. "Turning from battling the British, to out and out piracy against her own land and people – and not content with that, to foist his infamy upon us! 'Tis insufferable, not to be borne. From this day forth all else for us shall be secondary to hunting him down, to wreak upon him the retribution he so richly deserves! Crowd on more sail, Mr. Hubbard. Let us be about it."

FIVE

In succeeding days the hunt became an obsession with Mad Josh. Running down on every sail they sighted, with a bland indifference to who or what the ship might prove, veering away after their look, a dozen times in as many days they skirted disaster. Somehow they avoided it, disdaining prizes, refusing battle. It was a course which brought them even closer to the shores of England, since the trail of the *Lively Lady*, sailing still under false colors, led them there. Twice, hailing friendly flags, shouting across from deck to deck, they had word of her.

It was clear now that Poynter had no fear of the royal navy, whose ships he had set out originally to harass. His immunity to harm, coupled with his record, betokened that he had made a peace of sorts with them. It was even possible that he was hearing reports in turn, of the twin ship which had turned so assiduously to hunting him, determined on vengeance. By venturing close to English shores, he might find a greater measure of safety.

For them, such proximity was an added risk, but Mad Josh kept the *Savage* plunging ahead. It was apparent to all that his original madness was progressing, driving him as he drove his ship. No one cared. All were actuated by the common purpose.

Hubbard ventured a mild remonstrance as they moved by night, disdaining normal precautions. He had nothing to go on save his own calculations and an instinct which warned of disaster. "I can smell land," he said. "Belike England's somewhere off there, and we're getting in too close."

"I can hear no breakers," Mad Josh shrugged, a retort which disclosed all too well the set of his mind, strangely indifferent to normal precautions. "Nor can I see anything."

Again Hubbard was tempted to venture, to warn his captain to silence. There was a new quality to the night, sounds somehow familiar, increasingly ominous. Small noises, like the wash of waves against other ships; and apparently more than one. Aimless in night and fog, he had a notion that they had poked their bows into a hostile harbor, as any in this part of the world would prove.

A harbor in which enemy ships might be, all about –

Though there had been no order, the crew was alert, sharing his uneasiness. The trouble was that there was nothing to be done, lacking wind with which to move. Never had Hubbard wished so fervently for even a breath, despite what it might disclose.

He caught a sound, the strain and heave as wind filled a sail, but certainly not one of theirs. There was wind, and with it the fog was splitting apart, revealing, almost at point-blank range, another ship, its crew beginning to move. It was the *Lively Lady*, and across the brief span of water Hubbard was looking into the well-remembered face of Denny Poynter.

That Poynter shared his surprise registered across his startled face – recognition, followed in swift array by hate and triumph. Even as Hubbard shouted an order, Poynter was bellowing his own.

Mad Josh was writhing on the deck, clearly in the grip of a seizure.

SIX

Though the fog was lifting, the gusting wind was fluky, momentary. There was none to fill their sails, nothing to afford steerageway or allow them to maneuver. And chance had placed the *Lively Lady* in deadly position for attack – of which Poynter was moving to take advantage.

There was no time for Mad Josh, even had there been anything which he might do. Hubbard was thankful for an alert crew, jumping to his order, yet almost inevitably too late. A couple of the guns of the *Savage* managed to beat their rivals by a fraction, but at best that would be of little consequence, scarcely more than a gesture of defiance. Even as their sound rent the air, it was vibrating to the concussion of a broadside, delivered at point-blank range. The *Savage* staggered and heeled. An instant later, there was a far more devastating explosion.

Blinded and deafened, Hubbard was shakily aware of what was happening, even understanding. He was no longer on the deck of the *Red Savage*, but picked up and hurled as by a giant hand, while the ship disintegrated beneath. One of the cannon balls comprising the broadside, whether deflected or badly aimed, had penetrated to the *Savage*'s store of powder. It was a chance in a thousand; the one was sufficient. The *Savage* was blown apart, ripped in a welter of destruction.

Save that the echoing smash of sound was shut away, Hubbbard was hardly aware as the sea closed over him. The waters were black as the night, but buoyant. Hubbard fought his way to the surface, lungs snatching air from a surface choked with wreckage but suddenly, ominously silent. There were no screams from injured men, no wild threshing and struggling. In the half-light which hovered close above the water he could see no other swimmers.

A second breath of wind was following the first. Through the murkiness of dissipating fog he caught a glimpse of land, its mass dark but unmistakable, apparently no more than a mile or so distant.

Ironically, he seemed to be unhurt, apparently the only survivor of all who had sailed out from Connecticut. It was a strange and not too welcome prank of the luck which had dogged them these last days of Mad Josh's affliction. Not only was he alive while other good men were lost, but in the

31

moment of assuming his first command he had lost it.

And the vengeance for which Mad Josh had sought so frantically was all on the other side. Denny Poynter and his ship were virtually unscathed. It was his enemy who had been destroyed.

Again the wind had died, and its lack was a boon. The sea was scarcely ruffled, enabling him easily to keep afloat, aided by a bit of wreckage. With the steady lifting of the fog he was able to confirm his earlier guess, that they had reached not only the English shore but a harbor, that they had gotten right in among a lot of other vessels.

The tide was setting in. Aided by it, swimming easily, Hubbard made the shore and clambered on to dry land. He was some distance from the harbor, one of considerable size, filled almost to overflowing with the dark outline of ships. What had the loom of a town was some distance in an opposite direction.

He came to his feet, to stand swaying and unsteady. The earth seemed to pitch and roll like the deck of a ship, which he knew was the result of being so long away from such solidity.

On shore, a faint breeze struck chill through his soaked garments. Taking stock, he shook

32

his head at the caprices of fate. The shattering blast which had disintegrated the *Savage* had taken its toll from him. He was in his underwear, and even it showed scorched and torn. His outer garments, strangely including his shoes, had been stripped from him in total.

Only one possession remained. The money-belt which he always wore, prudently strapped about his waist, was intact. In it was a comfortable handful of gold coins. He would have to move prudently, a stranger in a strange country; worse, in enemy country. But gold was a universal sesame. He should be able to buy new clothes, food – It should see him through the initial part of a trying period, while he oriented himself and took stock. Many times, since Renee had set sail for these same shores, he had hoped to also reach English soil, but certainly not after such a fashion.

The loss of his clothes was more a boon than otherwise. Had he been found in the uniform of an American sea officer he would at the least suffer imprisonment for the duration of the war, or, very possibly, risk execution as a spy. Now there was nothing to link him to America or its navy, save perhaps his accent. His New England accent was English, but it would fall strangely on English ears.

Still, with a bit of caution and luck he should manage.

Perhaps repenting of the tricks it had played him of late, luck smiled in the next few hours. He found a small house, occupied by a fisherman and his family. They were accustomed to shipwreck, so his plight occasioned them no particular wonder. For one of the gold pieces, they supplied him with food and shelter, and clothes – garments well-worn, but that was an advantage.

"'Tis an ugly bit of water, out there, at times," his host assured him. "As who should know better than Oi, who've sailed and battled the seas all o' me loife. There was a toime 't was a fair easy loife, that o' a fisher, wi' not too many ships coming and going and the waters uncrowded. A toime so far back 't is hard to remember. But I'm Plymouth barn an' bred, and it's in Plymouth or the seas about her, na doubt, that I'll one day die."

Plymouth! Hubbard's pulse quickened at the name. Actually it was not too surprising, since the *Red Savage* had reached and made its way into a tricky harbor under such conditions, that it should be Plymouth. According to family tradition, some of his ancestors had embarked from Plymouth on an even chancier voyage, several generations before. What intrigued him was the report which had reached back, to the effect that the Marquis d'Ernee had found and purchased a home, somewhere out from Plymouth. If that was so, this was too good an opportunity to overlook. To see Renee once more, even if only for a little while – always he had cherished the hope.

Boyish eagerness, youthful promises, had been one thing, but he'd intended to make good on them, somehow. Chance was providing an opportunity. To seek them out might prove a risky venture, but hardly worse than what confronted him already. That Renee would welcome him he was sure. Her parents might be less enthusiastic, but for the sake of one-time friendship he was confident that they would not betray him.

It might be foolish, an adventure which at best could lead nowhere, still it would be worth the try. To see Renee once more, to hear the blithe cadences of her voice, to assure himself that all was well with her! Though he might argue contrarily in his mind, he'd known instantly that he would make the attempt.

Daylight revealed the mass of shipping stretched far out, across a choppy harbor. Activity of every sort connected with the sea, doubled in wartime, sprawled far beyond the confines of the former town. In many aspects it was similar to Connecticut, yet completely different, confusing yet reassuring. Among such a mass of humanity, no one was likely to waste a second look at him.

Reaching the town, he spent two more of his gold pieces in a shop, acquiring new clothes, a suit clean and respectable, if lacking in the elegance which might be appropriate when approaching so distinguished a family as the d'Ernees. Their estate, he learned, was half a score of miles out in the country, not too long a walk. Securing a shave, he smiled at such a thought. In his imagination he'd been eager to go, if necessary, to the ends of the earth to find Renee again.

The d'Ernees, it appeared, were still fugitives from their native land, but that situation would in all likelihood soon be corrected. In any case, they had salvaged quite a few of their possessions, and the Marquis was not merely a rich man, but a citizen of another world – even though in America he had been friendly and democratic. How much of that attitude had been genuine, how much a careful adaptability to circumstances over which he had no control, was another thought which as a boy had never occurred to Hubbard. But in supporting the ousted regime, they had been against everything which the new had espoused. To the Bourbon party, liberty and equality were anathema.

There was a considerable distance between the harbor and the town. Once past the town, the road which he followed was winding, the day warmly pleasant. The feel of solid ground, springy turf beneath his feet, after months at sea, was exhilarating. And here, like the town, no one gave him more than a passing glance.

SEVEN

Once he glimpsed the house, Hubbard was in no doubt that he had found the right place. A sprawling mansion of a house was set among large and well-kept grounds. Flowers and hedges interspersed the green of lawns. War had touched lightly here.

Had there been any room for doubt it was removed as he caught a glimpse of a petite little figure well back from the buildings. A door-like opening in an arbor disclosed a sun-dial. Bending pensively above it was Renee. Though more mature, she was a still elfin little creature, shading the dial with cupped hands as though to slow the advance of time. In that was the same suggestion of mischief as he remembered from games long since played. More than once, in hide and seek, she had eluded Denny Poynter, while permitting Hubbard to find her, one more shared secret.

Here, behind a hedge of trees, it was quiet and peaceful, though from off by the house someone was calling, a voice shrill with annoyance, ending in a breathless imprecation. At the bewilderment, an added spot of color washed Renee's cheeks. Hubbard saw the glint of excitement in her eyes as she stepped carefully behind the thicker screen of a bush.

"Renee!" he called.

Her eyes widened at sight of him, mouth rounding to a scarlet O. Startled as she was, her recognition was as instant as his own. She started forward, then glanced toward the house, the renewed voices which pleaded as well as quested. Eager welcome filled her eyes, replaced by the old glint of mischief. She placed a finger across her lips, then beckoned with a glance and led the way, to a spot still more sheltered. Beside him she was half on tiptoe, the subtle fragrance of her warm in his nostrils. "Bran! How utterly

38

incredible, but how completely like you!" Her English held the merest hint of accent. "Just when I was thinking of you, wishing so much that you might be here – even knowing how impossible that was –"

For all that she held her voice scarcely above a whisper, she spoke fast and eagerly. Her face held a blend of emotions, hope and eagerness mingled with welcome.

"You're alive!" she added, and her fingers touched his hand, a light caress, as though to make sure of the reality. "Just lately there have been such dreadful rumors, of a battle just off-shore, a ship which some claimed was the *Red Savage* destroyed, sunk, with no survivors! And weeks ago I heard of the *Red Savage*, out of Connecticut, and that you were one of the officers –"

They talked eagerly. Hubbard confirmed the truth of what she had heard, but giving few details beyond his own survival, followed by his determination, upon discovering where he was, to find her if possible, to fulfil that long-ago pledge. Renee listened, between a mixture of shock and ecstasy.

"To come so horribly close to death – how frightful! Oh, Bran! If you had been dead, I would have been almost reconciled to this other! In such a case, nothing would matter. But you are alive! Bother!" she added with sudden vehemence, as the voices approached still closer, calling her name. "I can't be found now – now more than ever – I won't –"

She drew him deeper into the shelter of the bushes as a maid went past, still half-pleading, as though convinced that her mistress must hear. Bran set an arm about her shoulders, feeling her tremble as a horseman came clattering at a wild pace on the road from town. The animal was dark with sweat, flecked with foam. Hubbard, surprised, made out the uniform of an officer of the King's navy, as the rider all but tumbled from the saddle.

"Captain Dupont," he gasped. "I have an urgent message for Sir Harry!"

Silently they watched as the newcomer was led toward the house, to be met half-way by a clearly enraged Sir Harry. Though invisible from where they stood, voices carried well. Sir Harry's was at once cold yet passionate.

What the message might be they could not make out, but he supplied the answer even while providing one for his officer.

"Of course I'll come!" He raised a shout which promptly produced a lumbering coach, driven by a liveried footman and drawn by four horses. Apparently they had waited in instant readiness for his summons. The Captain addressed himself to the gathered servants. "I'm called back to my ship – urgent. It's too bad that everyone had to be gone when I came – the Marquis and all his family, in especial the Lady Renee d'Ernee. Damned strange, in fact, not to say insulting. I make so wearing a trip out here to pay my respects –"

He broke off as though words failed, there was the slam of a door as he settled himself in the coach, then Hubbard had a glimpse of the equipage, rolling at a smart pace, rounding a curve of the grounds to the road, its clatter receding toward the distant town.

Captain Sir Harry Dupont was manifestly a person of importance, particularly in his own eyes. Almost unquestionably he commanded one of the ships in the harbor. That he had hired a coach and made his way here to pay his respects, at least as much to Renee as to the Marquis, was understandable.

But that he should find no one at home when he came – almost certainly unexpected and unannounced – was another matter. The lack of such a welcome as he had clearly anticipated had enraged him; the failure of the servants to find Renee, whom they must have reported as somewhere about the place, had further shortened an already bad temper.

To Hubbard's surprise, once the sounds died away, Renee's eyes were sparkling with

41

remembered mischief. "This is like the games we used to play, isn't it?" she breathed. "Only this time there would be the very devil to pay if they found me now. I'm being very naughty, and showing a terrible lack of hospitality, running away just when so distinguished a gentleman comes to pay his respects! I don't mean you, Bran," she added, and color flooded her cheeks. "I'd never run from you."

Elated though Hubbard was, the episode was worrisome. Only a great gentleman or a great lady could get away with such conduct. There might well be repercussions. But Renee drew an unrepentant breath.

"Thank goodness, the gentleman can take a hint – or at least the call of duty furnishes an excuse for injured dignity!" She nodded a pertly rounded chin. "I'm sure that no one aboard his ship ever dares to talk back or gainsay his slightest whim! It should be good for him, to discover that he's not omnipotent."

"Just who is he?" Hubbard asked curiously. Her answer took his breath.

"Captain Sir Harry Dupont, of the *Indefatigable*. I understand that his ship is in the harbor, and so of course the gallant captain was only doing his duty, being properly polite, in coming to pay his

42

respects to me as his intended bride. And I treat him so shamefully!" A small giggle escaped her.

Dupont of the *Indefatigable!* They had clashed outside Long Island Sound, a meeting which Captain Dupont must remember bitterly, not only with victory snatched away at the last moment but with *Racer* cut in two by his own vessel. In the stresses of battle there had been errors of judgment, probably on the part of both captains, and none of Dupont's memories could be other than bitter.

And Renee was saying that she was this man's promised wife – a political alliance beyond question, but doubly unthinkable. What she was saying was surprising, but in keeping with his memories of her as a child. Time had not quenched her irrepressible spirits or love of mischief.

The Lively Lady! Her glance was elfin, more delighted than repentant. He'd been thinking of Poynter, and suddenly, in the commander of the big frigate, was another, unexpected rival. The name meant nothing, but the shaken dignity which had been so apparent, the undoubted rage of Sir Harry, told a great deal. Should such a man ever find himself wedded to a woman like Renee, he'd be increasingly angry and baffled, faced with a problem of discipline beyond his control. Aboard ship he would rule with iron, and his inability to understand a woman would be unsettling.

Renee turned serious, though her eyes still danced.

"This is all because of this dreadful war, with all the politics which are involved," she explained. "Papa, as you know, is an important official of King Louis, and a firm defender of the Bourbon cause. Which makes us more or less allied with England, originally against revolutionary France, and since then against Napoleon.

"At least, that's the way everything has been for as long as I can remember. Lately of course it has been different, though it seems not quite real that so invincible a general was defeated, or that King Louis is in the process of being restored to his throne. And ourselves, once that happens, to our estates in France –"

Her nose wrinkled at this outline of benefits, in a pert gesture strangely like distaste. "But that of course is where politics become mixed with policy. You probably understand them as well as I do – and like them just as little. In such a game, the daughters of royalty or even of the nobility are played as pawns on international chessboards.

My Papa loves me dearly, but that makes no difference. I'm one of those pawns."

With a sense of increasing coldness, Hubbard was beginning to understand.

"Sir Harry, I am assured, has a distinguished record as a naval commander," Renee went on. "Also he comes of an old and fine English family. It has been devised by some of those who are working to put the old order back together in a new fashion, after so many years of disruption. France and England are supposed to be more deeply linked through my marriage to Sir Harry."

All of that was understandable, a practice hallowed by tradition. But in relation to Renee, it was like a nightmare, monstrous, impossible. That Renee should be bartered in such a fashion, for whatever reason –

"And so Sir Harry was calling here, just now, to pay his respects? As was right and proper, of course, chance or fortune having brought his ship to Plymouth. Think how offended I would have been had he failed to do so! It was a courtesy call, and I've no doubt he was looking forward to meeting me, to gain some notion of what his intended bride might be like; whether or not I was passably good-looking, tall or short, fat or thin –"

Hubbard's smile responded to the mischief in her own. "Then you've never met?"

"Today was our closest approach – and I managed a look at him! When I heard that he was at the front door, I slipped out of the house at the back and kept from sight, which was dreadfully discourteous, and of course the poor man's upset and furious. As I'm sure dear Papa will be. But I didn't want to meet him – not yet, at least. Those dreadful stories of the *Red Savage* had upset me. And if I hadn't been out here, I'd have missed you, Bran, and that would have been a calamity."

It developed that her parents, unaware of the impending call from the Captain, were absent for the afternoon, as was her brother Robert, who would have been even more scandalized and angry at such cavalier treatment on her part. Sir Harry, accordingly, had been met only by servants, who had been compelled to admit that Renee was somewhere about. But their efforts to find her at so critical a moment had been unavailing.

How much of that Captain Sir Harry Dupont had believed did not require much imagination. Manifestly he had been of the opinion that he had been grossly affronted. Undoubtedly, considering the youth and beauty of the wife he had been promised, her high social standing and the dowry she would bring, he would allow himself to be placated, but he had departed in a rage.

46

"Isn't it too bad that everyone should have chanced to be away when he came?" Renee sighed, her eyes adance. "Or that I should have been taking the air and wandered so far that I could not be found? But we have so few visitors – and how was I to guess that he might appear without warning?" She dismissed such difficulties with a gesture. "Tell me about yourself, Bran."

There was so much to talk about, so little time. They conversed eagerly, falling to sudden silences, each oppressed with the reality of the situation, the awareness that this visit was a brief interlude which could change nothing. He was a man without a ship, an enemy in a strange country. Even had he arrived as first officer of the *Red Savage*, somehow to be as well received as Poynter had been in the *Lively Lady*, what difference could it make?

The rumbling of another coach betokened that her parents were returning. She must be back at the house ahead of them, however surprised at what the servants would report, properly contrite. To fail to be there now would arouse suspicion that the other might have been less accidental than she protested.

"Oh, Bran – if only – my dear, you'll be careful –"

He resisted the desperate impulse to take .

47

her in his arms, to kiss her fears away, to reassure her. "I've got to go – for both our sakes," he said, and she caught the desperation in his tones. "I'll see you again – somehow – Renee."

He plunged away, and after a moment she was gone as well. There was nothing to do but get back to town, to think it through, to somehow evolve a plan.

Half a mile from the grounds he leaped quickly aside as another coach clattered suddenly over the top of a little hill and swept down at him. Four horses were panting under the whip, the lumbering vehicle filled with men – sailors, to his increasing astonishment – and on the seat beside the driver, staring back with as startled disbelief, rode Denny Poynter.

Poynter – also, unmistakably, on his way to pay a call upon Renee and her parents. As he too had promised one day to do.

EIGHT

Excitement painted colors rich and warm in Renee's cheeks. What a day it was proving to be, what a wonderful afternoon! Even better

48

than the news that Bransom Hubbard was alive had been seeing him, talking together. She felt equal to any explanations which might be required.

Slipping blithely in at a back door, she was almost instantly surrounded by a cordon of servants, exclaiming, questioning, explaining. So unfortunate that she should have been absent at such a time! The distressful rage of the so-gallant English captain, forced to take his leave without paying his respects, despite all their efforts to find her! Where – how –

Renee was surprised, enraptured, contrite, all at once. It was so delightful a day, and she had wandered farther than she had intended, so refreshing a stroll. But how was one to know, even to guess, with no word in advance, as would have been proper and to be expected under such a circumstance? Of course she understood that, with so little time at his disposal, Sir Harry had been unable to observe the customs of the French court. The whole affair, as they related it, appeared such a distressful mistake.

Her parents were equally upset, though it was her brother who blamed her for wandering away without explanation, for being absent when she should have remained at home. The worst of it was that there was fresh difficulty, added trouble, to add to the woes which had beset both England and the old order of the French for so long. What that was, the Marquis had been unable to discover. There was a pervasive breath of unease, a sense almost of doom. Almost certainly that had had something to do with Sir Harry's swift recall to his ship. If there was fresh trouble it would probably make it impossible for him to return – even if his lacerated pride might allow of such a course.

There were recriminations. In the midst of the confusion, Denny Poynter made his appearance.

He had looked forward to this visit as a pleasant interlude, possibly an opportunity, of which he would take whatever advantage might offer. The ride itself had proved unsettling. Twice he had glimpsed roadside scenes which had shaken and dismayed him. The half-formed plans with which he had set out were in disarray.

The initial surprise had been a glimpse of a man on foot, stepping quickly back into the shelter of trees and brush as the coach had approached. In that there was nothing out of the ordinary. Those who knew what was good for them, he reflected sardonically, would give a wide berth to any and all strangers. The startling aspect was that the fellow had looked like Bran Hubbard. Since Hubbard was dead, that was manifestly impossible, but it had been a nasty shock.

Minutes later, Poynter's coach had swerved to make way for the passage of another equipage of equal size. On its box, alongside the driver, aloof from the sailors who packed the interior, Poynter had recognized the elaborately splendid dress of a British naval captain.

Gossip had been rife in Plymouth, and some of it had reached his ears. The flow of reports concerning the French Marquis had been accelerated by a transfer of gold. Poynter had no trouble in understanding.

Unquestionably the Captain had been making a call at the estate, to pay his respects to the Marquis but most of all to Renee. There could be no one else of sufficient importance to draw him so far from his ship at such a time.

With an eye to business, he had taken along as many from his ship's crew as the coach would accommodate. Even as Poynter had filled his own, though from a motive which differed considerably.

It was clear enough, adding rumors and reports. This was the Englishman to whom Renee was to be given as a pawn in a political game; secondarily as a bride.

Poynter had his emotions under control, his

face schooled to impassiveness by the time he alighted and desired a menial to announce his arrival. One part of his mind was enjoying the effect which that announcement would create. He could picture the surprise, mingled with bewilderment at such a display of arrogance on his part. They would of course remember him, those recollections influenced by his spreading reputation, which he had no doubt would have reached even here. At best it was a mixed bag, a highly successful voyage if considered solely in the light of ships seized or sunk, battles won or more often secured by surprise –

The word treachery, as applied to himself, Poynter excluded from his vocabulary. Initiative had a better sound. And there might be room for its exercise before the day was over.

Having heard of his activities, they would certainly count it as effrontery for him to present himself. He was right. There were the emotions he had prepared for, a chill hauteur predominating. Only in Renee's face, after the initial surprise, was there a startled foresight, a flash of apprehension.

Poynter's breath caught at sight of Renee, to the exclusion of other thoughts. Even as a maid she had been beautiful, and that promise had been more than fulfilled with maturity.

Poynter's half-formed resolution altered to certainty. It had been no more than youthful boastfulness that, as a man, he'd find her and carry her away. But at this fresh sight of her, her remembered loveliness enhanced, he was on fire for her. And with a multiplicity of events crowding, there would be no second chance. It was the only way.

Already he had cast discretion to the winds, and it had paid off. Perhaps also he owed a reasonable show of gratitude to this land where now he was accepted; but it was no more than toleration, in those circles where he had hoped to move as something of a hero; men like Sir Harry Dupont had already made clear that in selling his birthright he'd acquired a mere mess of pottage in exchange. Glances and words, carefully polite, relegated him to a position too low for contempt. But he'd show them, make good that boyish boast to find her and carry her away. The sight of Hubbard had shaken him. The added presence of Sir Harry rendered action imperative.

Poynter knew that he had to have her, and it had to be now. He must put to sea again in any case, and the situation allowed of no procrastination.

To Poynter they remained coldly polite. Since he had made himself a guest in their

53

house, and for the remembrance of days when as children he and Renee had played together, he was tolerated. They asked a few questions, tactfully phrased, concerning his expedition as a privateer, the ship he commanded. Its name they carefully avoided.

Their distaste, as he recognized with mounting rage, was of a matching quality with that of the English. In a world at war they tolerated a turncoat who assisted them, going to necessary lengths to encourage such defection. But never would they accept him as an equal. Had anything been lacking to cement his hardening resolution, it was the clear evidence of their contempt. Well, he'd bring down that haughty pride, and tame the haughty lady in the process. Since he had the name of pirate, he might as well have the game.

He'd marry her, of course – if for no other reason than her wealth and connections, which could be of increasing importance to him.

Poynter played his part with secret elation. He shook his head gravely as the situation was unfolded.

"I've never had the pleasure of meeting Sir Harry, but I've heard a great deal about him," he observed. "One of the more successful captains in the royal navy, his career increasingly distinguished. Almost certainly he'll be an admiral at some not distant day. How highly unfortunate that you should have been absent when he called, Miss Renee. These English, if you'll excuse the observation, are confoundedly arrogant. To say nothing of a matching pride. It would be too bad if such a combination of mischances should lead to further misunderstanding."

Renee's brother, even her parents, listened with increasing approval. Poynter pursued gravely. "I don't know exactly what's afoot, but all day, there's been a stir through the ships in harbor and in Plymouth. What seems to be a growing unrest, along with a spate of rumors. Something is certainly up. Any such unrest, fresh trouble, is certain to affect Sir Harry, to require him to take to sea again, probably without delay, and for who can guess how long –"

"His departure was hastened by the arrival of a messenger, with some news which threw him into a frenzy," the Marquis elaborated. The butler had detailed that in full.

Poynter spread his hands in wide dismay.

"As I feared! And once his ship puts to sea, it will be too late! It's a double shame that a misunderstanding should exist, but it would be still more unfortunate to allow it to persist, to assume undue magnitude with the passage of time." He became suddenly decisive.

"I too, will have to be on the move. That becomes a virtual certainty. But, fortunately, I am a more or less independent agent, not subject to orders from the Admiralty. As a one-time neighbor and, I hope, friend, I may perhaps be of at least a small service in helping to set matters right, before the opportunity is lost. To you –" he bowed to each in turn, most sweepingly to Renee – "it would be a small payment on a debt of long standing. And should it serve to promote good-feeling between allies, at so critical a moment –"

He paused a moment, then outlined his plan.

"I came well escorted, with men from my ship, deeming that the unsettled state of affairs required such prudence. I would esteem it an honor to proffer my coach and my men as a bodyguard to escort Miss Renee to Plymouth, immediately. If I could be furnished with a good riding horse –" he glanced tentatively at the Marquis, who, though not understanding, nodded.

"I may perhaps be able to precede them by a little, to present myself to Sir Harry at his ship, to in some degree explain, so that by the time Renee reaches the town, he could meet her at some proper hostelry which you may suggest, to brush aside misunderstandings. That she would make such a gesture would resolve all doubt or ill-feeling from his mind –"

Robert d'Ernee's mind had already run ahead. If what Poynter suggested was somewhat unprecedented, so too were the circumstances. "The Angel Inn – a bite of supper, together – we will all be greatly indebted to you, Captain Poynter."

"It is a notion of merit," the Marquis admitted. "We could accompany you, my dear –"

Poynter lost no time in nipping such a notion in the bud. "With all deference, sir, but would that be wise? Might it not appear to make too much of what was, after all, only an unfortunate misunderstanding? It would almost be to put you and Miss Renee in the wrong. Let her go properly escorted, by all means – accompanied by Robert, with her maid and perhaps his servant. That way the courtesy is returned, no more."

For almost the first time, the Marquis was favorably impressed by this Yankee captain, despite the tales which circulated concerning him. But such stories, he knew, had a way of becoming magnified out of reason.

"There is merit in what you say. Renee will of course spend the night at the Angel. In the morning, I will assemble a proper escort, and come after her. That way, all will be managed with proper form and decorum. We are indebted to you, Captain Poynter."

Poynter's breath of relief was checked an instant later. To the surprised dismay of all the rest, Renee was not disposed to go along.

NINE

"Why should I rush to town to show abjectly before this English captain, when he left with such discourteous remarks concerning not only me but the rest of you?" Renee countered. "That I was not here to receive him was unfortunate, that I grant. But the fault is not one-sided. To rush to appease him would make it appear so, implicating me in guilt."

There was at last a measure of truth in what she said. After all, though Sir Harry was a rising captain in the service of his king, neither in wealth nor social position did he match the d'Ernees of Bourbon France. It was a matter of the utmost delicacy.

Poynter was dismayed. He had planned

boldly, and everything had seemed to be going smoothly – too much so, he reflected ruefully. When luck smiled over-warmly, it was apt like wind in a storm at sea to veer sharply the next instant. He eyed Renee sharply. She was far too innocent, wide-eyed and thoughtful – and always, at such a time, as he had discovered to his cost; a minx, that wily brain beneath so lovely an exterior adroit at plotting mischief.

Fortunately he had the means to answer her. Her absence when Sir Harry had called, with all efforts on the part of the servants to locate her unavailing –

Events might fall out in such fashion, but he did not for an instant believe that they had. Hubbard – devil take the man – had been ahead of both Dupont and himself. While Sir Harry had been cooling his heels, she had been with Hubbard –

That explained everything, and jealousy stabbed Poynter like a resharpened conscience. He had assured himself, across the lengthening years, that her liking for Bransom Hubbard had been no more than a girlish infatuation, certain to wear away, to be forgotten. For himself, he had been sorely smitten by her charms, and the years had strengthened rather than diminished the intensity of feeling.

Unquestionably, it had been the same between Hubbard and Renee.

She had loved Hubbard then, and she loved him still. His jealousy at least furnished a clearer insight. Of course she had heard the calls and been aware how the servants were searching, knowing that Sir Harry was waiting impatiently for a sight of his promised bride. Coolly perverse, she had allowed the affront to develop as it might.

Despite his fury, he could not but admire her. Whatever the abhorrence of her parents and the Bourbon faction, she, like many of her generation, had imbibed something of that spirit of liberty, equality and fraternity for which so much blood had been shed. Undoubtedly her sojourn in America had enhanced her liking for democracy. Given a taste of liberty and equality, she had developed independence.

France to her was a foreign land, King Louis as much a pretender as the Corsican. International intrigues might occupy such of the nobility as her father, left otherwise without purpose. To her those plottings were largely meaningless, often foolish. And that she should be made a pawn on such a board, she found increasingly distasteful.

Poynter could understand, at least to a degree. But he had a tool to counter that.

"There is one other matter," he said gravely. "I have hesitated to speak of it, for the distress which it might cause you, knowing how high was the esteem in which you held Bransom Hubbard, years ago. But now that I have had time to think over what I saw on my way out here, to place events in perspective, I am afraid that Hubbard is in grave danger."

"What do you mean?" The exclamation was torn from Renee, as if against her will. "Bran –"

Poynter was blunt.

"Not far back, I glimpsed him beside the road, on foot. At first I was incredulous, not believing it possible that it could be him. But I know now that it was. He ducked from sight, and my driver did not stop. But almost at once, I met another coach, headed toward Plymouth – it could only have been Sir Harry's. There was a distant outcry and confusion, and I've just realized what must have happened. The unrest and disturbance can only mean that the press gangs are out, ranging even this far inland. Sir Harry, of course, like all English shipmasters, finds himself short-handed as he is ready to put to sea. The presence of so many of his sailors, under an officer, in his coach is explained. They were along to act as a press gang."

61

The sudden paleness of Renee's face told him that no further explanation was needed. Glimpsing Hubbard, they must have pursued and caught him before he was aware of danger.

Final persuasion was not difficult. With her lover in danger, pride took second place. Poynter was well satisfied.

Poynter's blend of fact with fiction had a reasonable sound. Realizing now that it was Hubbard whom he had seen, the rest might have happened. For his purpose the suggestion proved sufficient. Renee was persuaded to make the journey to Plymouth.

Hubbard checked a headlong pace, startled in turn at sight of Poynter, instantly realizing what it implied. He was half-minded to go back, then changed his mind, since Poynter could hardly be a threat to Renee. His boyish boast had been to find Renee and carry her away, but the hazards of such an attempt would almost certainly deter him from so wild a notion. Already, his conduct aboard the *Lively Lady* had placed him in bad repute with his own countrymen, and hardly better with others. To infringe the hospitality of the British, after purchasing a working partnership at such cost, would render him outcast, with nowhere to turn.

That he should make use of an opportunity

to visit Renee was entirely in keeping. It matched the coincidence that all three of them, who might be described as her suitors – Poynter, Sir Harry and himself – should chance to come calling on the same day.

His own bad luck might have certain advantages. Poynter and Sir Harry would have little time before they were forced to put to sea again. But he had nowhere to go, and all the time in the world. He might return another day.

A file of men on the road ahead caught his attention. Like himself, they were headed for town, moving purposefully. But they were almost as alien to this section of rural England as himself. Each wore the uniform of the royal navy. One or even a pair of sailors might venture inland for business or pleasure, but so many, with an officer at their head, were strangely out of place.

"Something's afoot," Hubbard reflected, and, recalling the uneasy expectancy which had seemed to grip the town, there seemed only one convincing answer, yet one contradicted by circumstances – a press gang.

That could explain all the oddities, including Sir Harry's being hastily summoned back to his ship. A canny shipmaster, he had probably been prepared for such a recall and what it implied, so had decided on such a journey to combine business with pleasure. He had loaded the coach with these men from his crew, watched, indeed guarded by officers, ready at notice to set about a business familiar for nearly a score of years in inhabitants near and surrounding all English ports – that of a press gang.

By bringing them farther inland than was the custom, ready to strike without warning, they might surprise a fair number of natives, seizing them wherever found, changing them as by the stroke of a magic wand from landlubbers to sailors, recruits for His Majesty's navy.

Actually the process was not so simple. A farmer or cobbler, who probably had never set foot even in a small boat, was transformed slowly and painfully into a seaman. Painful alike to the officers to whom the training was entrusted, but still more to the bewildered and unhappy recruits who, seized without warning, were hustled aboard ship, inducted under discipline during a brief ritual which they neither understood nor were allowed to question, much less resist. But once impressed into the royal service, men learned their new trade – or died in the process.

Over the years, warring not only against Napoleon but against most of the maritime world, the British navy had chronically found itself short-handed; the impressment of man-power when a ship touched at a port was nothing new. Aware of such practices, men went warily, keeping out of sight at such times.

The surprising part was that a discontinued practice should be happening now. With the fall of the Corsican and the removal of France and her navies from the adversary list, the English ships had found themselves with an over-supply not alone of ships but of manpower.

Something of import was happening. The press gangs were out again.

As if to supply proof, the men ahead debouched from the road, filtering through a gap in a hedge, to where the thatched roof of a farmhouse showed grayly from a cluster of trees. They had spied a man at work, at a moment when he had put it aside to return the smile of a girl who had ventured from the house.

The attention of the sailors was at least as much for the girl as the man, and that was understandable at first glance. Rustic though she might be, she was as slender and dainty as any of her city cousins, poised suddenly like a startled bird as the sailors came hurrying, bare head upflung.

Hubbard, more distant, was unable to see

her face clearly, but had he not known otherwise he must have been betrayed into supposing that she was Renee. Not alone in build and grace of movement, but even in the way she held her head, she too could have served as a model for the figurehead which graced both the *Red Savage* and the *Lively Lady*.

His back to the hurrying catchpolls, the man had eyes only for her. In the moments before she described them, it was apparent that she was as eager to bestow a kiss as to receive it. Then she started suddenly, backing a pace, her eyes widening with terror as she and her companion were surrounded, retreat cut off.

Not too willingly, the sailors were obeying the order to grab her companion. The officer lost no time in seizing her in turn. She cried out wildly as his arms encircled her.

Both captives struggled desperately, the man striking out blindly against the five, the girl with equal frenzy. Hubbard heard the tear of cloth, caught a glimpse of white flesh as her blouse tore, to the rough laughter of her captor.

"Easy now, girl," he protested. "If it's kisses you're bestowin', then I'm the man both to receive and return them, and if it's comfortin' you require, once that great lout

66

is taken away, sure it's comfort I can furnish in plenty!"

Jovial though his tone, his eyes glared avidly, and she cried out painfully as he jerked her closer, catching both her wrists in one great paw. The next instant he staggered, spun half about, as completely surprised in turn, to the savage clutch of Hubbard's fingers, a twisting wrench on his arm which sent him to his knees.

TEN

Hubbard's intervention was purely emotional, though as always when the time came for action one part of his mind was detached and cool. These sailors represented Sir Harry Dupont, in his present mood reason enough for thwarting them. That the girl bore so striking a resemblance to Renee played its part, almost as though it was an attack on her.

Startled by the unexpectedness of it, the officer came roaring to his feet, snatching for his sword and lunging, in a single continuous movement. The speed of his reaction favored him, but the blade was a mistake. Its lunging thrust was completely murderous, but

Hubbard took one backward step, bending his knees. The sword missed neck and shoulder, and the extremity of effort left its holder bent forward on his toes, unable to recover before Hubbard closed fingers about the wrist. His lift and heave became a continuation of the same effort.

Blastic's momentum completed what Hubbard initiated. A wild yell broke from him as he sprawled full-length, striking heavily, to lie gasping, the weapon spun from his grasp. Gazing up dazedly, he became aware that its point pricked his throat, a sinewy hand higher at the hilt, while beyond that, eyes glared in turn.

Then, to the unbelieving incredulity of each, Hubbard was collapsing, going down dazedly in turn. Blastic's eyes followed the rock which, bouncing from Hubbard's head, stirred a small coil of barnyard dust.

Understanding drifted slowly, like fog above the water. Hubbard came to an elbow, lifting his head at the giggle of laughter, to stare incredulously at the yokel who had thrown the rock from the shelter of an outbuilding. Staring foolishly, delighted with himself, if was clear that he had been motivated only by a desire to get in the fight, not by animosity. But such witless intervention had turned the tables.

"Grab him," Blastic growled, and came to his feet. *"Him,* you fools," he added, as a couple seized the yokel as well. For the timely assistance he disdained even a word of thanks, clearly assessing the man as a trouble-maker. "We don't want him," he emphasized. "Let him go."

With the mass of them piling atop him, Hubbard was secured. Then Blastic's rage broke forth anew as he discovered that the girl had availed herself of the opportunity to vanish. The officer swung back at Hubbard, manifestly more disappointed at that than all the rest.

"You stinking, interfering frog!" The epithet, reserved for the French, betrayed the extent of his hate. Hubbard, shakily regaining his feet, staggered to the smash of knuckles hard-driven. For an instant it appeared that Blastic would follow the blow with a further hail. Instead, catching sight of his sword, he snatched it up, as more deadly. Then, at the sheer horror in the faces of his men, a gleam of cunning steadied him.

"Bring them along," he growled, indicating the farmer who had been their initial objective, but with his attention centered on Hubbard. Anticipation had replaced the glare. He mouthed the thought.

"We've ways of dealing with your kind,"

69

he promised. "Once we have you aboard ship, you'll discover what a mistake it was to strike an officer of the King's navy."

He stood an instant longer to glare about, as if minded to make a search of the house and outbuildings. But clearly that would be a waste of time. The half-wit who had so muddled events watched them go, the momentary excitement in his eyes replaced by a habitual vacancy.

Hubbard's mouth held the taste of blood, but however unpleasant the situation, he was only too grimly aware that the future would be worse. His fellow-captive gazed wildly, increasingly dismayed as the full implication of what was happening was made clear. He swayed and stumbled, recovering with a frantic scramble at the prick of Blastic's sword. Blood reddened the torn cloth.

Their escort maintained an uneasy silence, in keeping with the mood of their officer. A mile had been covered before the bewildered countryman ventured a question of Hubbard.

"What are they takin' us for?" he asked. "This is a press gang. But I thought the bloody Corsican was a prisoner off somewhere."

One of the guards, apparently with memories of a similar plight, explained sympathetically.

"He was, but there's a report that he's escaped. Sounds that w'y, for sure. And if it's so, then the whole blarsted thing's to be done all over agyne."

Hubbard had been wondering if something of the sort had happened. It might be nothing more than rumor, but in any case it had come at a bad moment for potential press victims no longer on the alert. That fresh conflict with the French would to some extent reduce the pressure against the States would be the only benefit. The over-all situation would revert to what it had been when the *Red Savage* had slipped out from its moorings and down the Sound, to make its escape under cover of blackness and tempest.

Such news explained this disaster which had overtaken them along the way. The renewed press gangs, like Blastic's threat, were a portent of things to come. At best it was bad enough for fresh and unwilling recruits to be forced to serve under such an officer. But to start a voyage as the objects of his active hate –

With forced induction into the British service would vanish any hope he had entertained for somehow aiding Renee. His notions on that subject had been vague, but as a free agent, something might be contrived. But now –

For as long as the war lasted, he would be compelled to fight, and this time against his own side. Protest or any attempt at explanation would be ignored, though anything which he could say would serve only to blacken his case. Once aboard ship, any infraction of the rules, or a try at escape, would result at the mildest in an application of the cat to bared back; at a captain's order a recalcitrant sailor might be flogged through the fleet – at least as long as life remained inside a tortured body.

His fellow prisoner's mind was clearly inflamed by tales of such treatment.

"This can't really be happenin'," he protested wildly. "I'm dreamin' it. And Nora – what'll become of her? We was just married – only last week –"

"But at least, she got away," Hubbard reminded.

"Yes, thanks to you. But my poor girl! Not to see her ag'yn, not for years, maybe never – it can't be happenin'."

Blastic had been striding well ahead, but all at once he had fallen back, in time to overhear the plaint. His smile was akin to a shark's.

"Happens it is," he taunted. "Though this ain't but a tyste to what will happen to the pair of you, once you're aboard ship. I'll see to that. As for your woman, don't worry but what one as pretty as her'll find plenty of others to kiss her in your plyce. As I'd have done –"

He broke off as they came suddenly upon another luckless wayfarer and he was swept up, dragged along despite his protests. Abject terror rendered his muscles so flabby that he could barely walk, as he realized his predicament, envisioning what lay ahead. Hubbard could picture the reality for landsmen when, at sea, they were forced to ascend to the topmost rigging of a vessel pitching and wallowing to the blast of a gale, to spread sails or take them in, while clinging desperately to narrow stays or icy ropes, the black sea far out below.

One of the press gang staggered to the burst of a clod of dirt alongside his head, flung from sheltering brush. All at once the column was beset, more clods and stones coming from both sides, amid a chorus of cries and imprecations. In return there was only glimpses of figures, men and women alike, scurrying from clump to tree, a furious harrying.

Hubbard caught a glimpse of the girl Nora, and understood. She had run to a neighbor's, others roused in turn. At the tale of outrage, the settlers within reach were dropping everything to swarm to the attack, to attempt a rescue. Bonaparte might again menace England, and they placed their trust in the British navy, heroes all so long as they remained safely afloat. But the lawless seizure of one of their own, an attack on his wife by a press gang, was immediate and different.

This presented a rare chance for sport, a holiday of sorts on the part of the growing mob, moreover such a response was insurance against being surprised in similar fashion. Swearing frenziedly, Blastic could only hustle his column along at a faster clip, guarding their trio of captives, helpless to retaliate. He dared not order his men to shoot. What they were about, though accepted, was precarious, going largely unchallenged only because the country was at war. In any case, there were no targets at which to aim.

The harassment increased as they neared the town. Sticks, stones, vegetables – some snatched fresh and rock-hard from gardens along the route, but some half-rotten, even a dead cat, were among the assortment cast their way, to the discomfiture of prisoners as well as guards. But discipline prevailed, bolstered by the threat of muskets and pistols should the attackers venture into the open. Hot and disheveled, reeling with weariness, they staggered into the outskirts of Plymouth, and the others drew back. Strangely, there had been no other traffic along the road, neither carts nor coaches.

Hubbard had quickly recovered from his initial discomfiture, and was in better case than most of the others, though not by much. A couple of times he had been on the verge of making a break for it, to run at any cost, thwarted once as Nora's man was hit by a rock, a glancing blow which staggered him back against Hubbard. Instinctively he lent his support until his companion could recover, and by then the opportunity was lost.

They tramped through the town, eyed askance, given a wide berth. Men like Blastic might relish the role, but most detested such duty, and were scorned in turn. Darkness was closing around them, blotting away the buildings, the distant harbor and glimmer of sea in the last reflections of sunset. The heat of the desperate march was tempered by an insweeping wind.

The town was almost behind, the harbor showing darkly in the distance, when for a second time they staggered to the sudden fury of attack.

This time it was better planned. The countrymen clearly had neither given up nor withdrawn, hurrying instead to get ahead, gaining additional recruits. Under the closing night they ran no great risk. This time they struck silently, wielding clubs and knives. In the gloom it was difficult to distinguish between prisoners and guards. Hubbard's unhappy companion went to his knees, and Blastic, enraged, leaped toward them with drawn sword. Rather than risk an escape, he prepared to cut them down.

Another face loomed suddenly, agonized with sudden terror – that face so strangely like Renee's, desperate for her man. Hubbard fairly flung him into her arms, and the next instant the attackers were fading in the darkness. And none too soon, as local police came hastening to the succor of the faltering column.

ELEVEN

Staggered by the glancing clout of Blastic's sword, skull throbbing, Hubbard plodded mechanically until the lap and splash of waves were before them, a longboat waiting, drawn up on the beach. A pair of sailors roused from sleep, sprung to action. Clearly they had been set to watch each other as much as the boat through the long afternoon. That was in keeping with practice and discipline.

No time was lost in herding the trio of prisoners aboard, then the others grasped the oars almost with relief. The sea by comparison was suddenly friendly. Blastic, at the tiller, glowered at Hubbard, but held his temper in check.

Hubbard grimaced at the irony. He was going out to a ship, being rowed as befitted an officer, rather than toiling at the oars. His last not too similar boarding had been as mate of the *Red Savage*.

Another angle had a grimmer side. The water showed black, so that, with the moon still below the horizon, the entire harbor was a matching pool. Against it the silhouettes of distant ships were barely discernible, though here and there shaded lights marked their position. Specks which made the surrounding night heavier. Plymouth, equally distant, was no better.

But another boat had loomed close alongside as they were embarking, a lantern casting long shadows but a flash of light. In that gleam he had made out the ship's name, lettered on the side of the longboat. *Indefatigable.*

It came as no surprise, though the confirmation was less than pleasant. Here was the supreme irony, to be shanghaied aboard Sir Harry's vessel, which from every indication of the afternoon and the stir attendant aboard it, was all but ready to put to sea. Should Captain Dupont suspect the real identity of this recruit, a grim situation could become even more involved.

And if in so bedraggled an addition he envisioned a rival for his Lady's favor, or that Hubbard had been accorded precedence while he was left to cool his heels –

But there was no reason, no chance that he could possess a second sight. On the other hand, Hubbard's chances for possible escape had been lost, and he was doubly guarded.

The massive side of the double-decker loomed above. Hails were exchanged, then the trio of recruits were ordered to scramble up to the deck. A trio reduced to the two, since the escape of the farmer. The man ahead made hard work of the ascent, cursed and hoisted from below, to flop gaspingly on to the solidity of the deck.

A bosun grunted approvingly as Hubbard came easily, recognizing a sailor. In that was small satisfaction. All else aside, to be demoted from first officer of a privateer to the forecastle of a British man o' war was not at all to his liking.

He and the other were herded to join a dozen other uneasy men, the sweepings of other presses. Momentarily there was a

78

chance to look about. This was his first time aboard a ship of the royal navy, but he was familiar enough with similar vessels to appreciate the size and power of the seventy-four. By comparison, existence above the *Indefatigable* could be better than in some of the smaller, crowded craft with which England patrolled the seas.

He was swiftly aware of tenseness, an air of expectancy. With the sudden return of all-out war, the reversal of many ships of France from friend to foe, they were ready for duty. He guessed that *Indefatigable* awaited only the arrival of her captain before hoisting anchor. Sir Harry's abortive excursion inland had delayed him, though he had responded promptly to the receipt of the news carried by the messenger.

And somewhere, in this well-populated harbor, more than likely, the *Lively Lady* would also be lying. Poynter's presence on shore assured that. And for him there would be no great rush to duty.

A pair of petty officers were eying the recruits, discussing whether to immediately take them below and properly swear them in. In such matters the British were meticulous. The legal formality must be followed without deviation. After the ceremony, men would no longer belong to themselves, but as seamen be subject to rules and regulations. And more importantly, to naval discipline.

Until the swearing in, they could be seized without warning, hustled like slaves, but must be manhandled no more than necessity dictated.

Yet, by all reports, life aboard a British vessel was preferable to that in any other navy, excepting only the American, with their still strange and unacceptable notions of the rights of man. Even the French, following the revolution, had reverted under the Corsican to long-accepted practices. Only aboard American vessels did concepts of freedom prevail, notions which British officers accounted dangerous to the point of treason.

Sounds indicated that another boat had pulled alongside. From the stir and sudden twittering of the boatswain's pipes, Hubbard deduced that the captain was coming aboard, to be received with proper honors. He made Dupont out, brisk but square and beefy, the early moon picking out the same bulldog face that he had seen distantly through the telescope. Dupont's jaw was set in uncompromising bitterness, as though this rare excursion on to solid ground had proved as unsettling as first steps after being long at sea.

Unnoticing his captain's humor, a younger

80

officer approached, smirking, addressing Dupont with a certain degree of familiarity, clearly presuming on whatever circumstances had led to that shore expedition.

"Good hunting, I trust, Sir Harry?" he asked. "Fair lady as overjoyed as surprised at so unexpected a visit, eh?"

Another officer scowled, but the warning was too late. The bulldog jaw set a little harder.

"Your trust is as misplaced as your levity, my Lord," the Captain grunted, and the presumption was explained. Though a junior officer, a nobleman, particularly if young and inexperienced, might permit himself certain liberties. "Her Ladyship was not at home. And jouncing for a score of miles in these damned springless coaches is not my idea of a pleasure trip!"

"Of course, the Lady Renee d'Ernee would have had no intimation that the *Indefatigable* was in port, or that you would be paying her the compliment of a call," another officer intervened pacifically. "Had she known that Sir Harry Dupont was bestowing such an honor –"

Whatever else he might be, Sir Harry was forthright. He brushed the suggestion aside impatiently.

"Nonsense! No doubt the Lady accounts

the honor to be on the other foot, and rightly. After all, I'm only an English captain, and she the daughter of a Marquis. That the powers that be should see fit to cement an international alliance, with her Ladyship and my poor self as instruments, is an honor for me, but she may regard it in a different light. I missed seeing her, or any of her family. Even so far in the country, there seemed a great amount of confusion and distraction." He turned to more immediate and practical matters. "How many recruits were secured?"

"Nineteen, sir. The last were brought aboard just ahead of yourself –" a wave of the hand indicated where the unwilling nineteen awaited their fate.

Sir Harry was sufficiently interested to move nearer, to survey them with expert if disparaging eye. Momentarily his attention centered on Hubbard, half a head taller than the rest, with an air setting him apart as surely as the Captain's from his officers. Hubbard returned the stare. He had increasing reason for interest in this captain, with fate seeming to throw them mockingly across each others' paths.

Those bluntly revealing remarks had added considerably to what Renee had already told him. Hubbard knew that he had never quite realized the full truth before, even with riper

82

years and experience. In Connecticut, the d'Ernees had been neighbors, only their nationality and exile setting them apart, where one man was as good as another.

Now it was all too clear that the Marquis d'Ernee was of international stature. Probably his confiscated estates in France had been in the process of being restored to him through the joint efforts of the Bourbons and of England, who had supported the deposed Louis while warring with his usurper.

King Louis' return to his throne, like a lot of other plans, would again be in abeyance with the return of Napoleon, but the importance of such rich and influential a man in the continuing contest was in no degree lessened. If decades of struggle had impoverished France, England had suffered no less. An international alliance, consummated by a marriage between an eligible English sea captain and the daughter of the Marquis, was clearly desirable by the diplomats of both nations.

Such a marriage had been arranged, with the principals having little to say, beyond consenting. With Sir Harry at sea, they had never set eyes upon each other, an omission which Dupont, when the opportunity had offered, had sought to correct.

For his part, Captain Sir Harry Dupont

was the sort of career officer who would interpose no obstacles to the wishes of his government in such a matter, particularly with the prospect of a young and comely bride, along with an advancement in his fortunes, political as well as financial.

As for Renee – sweet, gay little Renee – no longer a girl, but a woman, by tradition scarcely more than a pawn in affairs of importance – her father would of course have consulted her, but taking her consent as automatic. That she might entertain notions of her own would be inconceivable. As for lingering memories of a boyhood swain, if indeed she still cherished such, they must be recognized as no more than a dream, impossible from the outset.

Dupont showed middle-aged, bluff in the best tradition of the service; with the wealth and prestige of such an alliance he could expect to become in due course an admiral and a baronet.

With increasing practicality, Hubbard had long since recognized a boyish dream for what it was, and unlikely ever to be more. Yet that Renee should be the intended bride of such a man, with no real voice in the matter – a man old enough to be her father, trained in the harshness of naval command, certain to be unyielding both in ideas and habits –

The renewal of the war was causing a delay, but Renee was in almost desperate need of help – and where else could she turn for it?

Denny Poynter's long-ago boast that when the time came it would be he who would carry her away, snatching her from all rivals – luck or chance had brought him to hand to complete the triangle. Over the years, that claim had rankled, made worse when Hubbard had faced Poynter across a narrow strip of water, with the realization that, now a turncoat and traitor, Poynter was accepted, accorded a haven even among English ships of war –

As between English captain or pirate turncoat, Hubbard could find small enough choice. Though for solid, honest manhood, Sir Harry must rank first. An officer growled an order as the Captain turned away, command for the recruits to step below. Once there, they would be speedily inducted into the royal service, allowed neither to ask questions or to voice a protest; neither could be permitted. And once it was accomplished, the authority and discipline of the navy would take over.

And with it, the vengeance which Blastic had promised to exercise.

Once that door closed, all chance would be lost. Hubbard ducked and ran, the suddenness of his move taking the others by surprise. He reached the rim of the deck and jumped, a reflected gleam of light marking the dark waters below. But waters which had proved not too unfriendly after an even more impromptu descent from the remnants of the *Red Savage*.

He struck feet first, and the bay seemed bottomless as he descended, the pressure on his lungs increasing with the depth. Then he was swimming, fighting back toward the surface, gulping air as his head broke water.

Already, on the deck above, there was outrage and frenzied activity, orders being roared to lower boats and initiate a hasty patrol. It was not that anyone aboard the *Indefatigable*, least of all her captain, would be overly concerned as to whether he drowned or otherwise perished. A single recruit, under such circumstances, was of small concern.

But for anyone to escape them, to desert – such actions would be a threat to discipline, to be discouraged at all costs. If he was brought back dead it would serve as well as alive, but returned he must be. And if alive, to an enduring regret that he had not died instead.

TWELVE

Hubbard scarcely needed even to tread water. To keep afloat in protected waters was almost mechanical. He looked about, making out several misty hulks, not anxious to move until the excitement should abate. It was an indication of his recklessly improving mood that he managed a grin at his own expense. He was pretty much back where he'd been after the destruction of the *Red Savage*, only more so. The overall situation was even less promising.

There was a stir, at least in this particular part of the harbor, a subdued yet half-frenzied activity. Small boats were out there, and such excitement was out of proportion to his escape. The dark outlines of two craft came nearer, the backs of both sets of oarsmen to each other, the steersmen perhaps confused or incautious. Someone exclaimed sharply as they almost collided, then mutual recriminations were exchanged – suddenly interrupted by a higher-pitched cry, the gasping voice of a woman.

"Help! Oh, help! I'm being abducted –"

The sound was cut off as abruptly as it

had come, as from a hand clapped over the unruly mouth, together with sounds of struggle. Hubbard strained to see or hear. It seemed a trick of the imagination – what else could it be, with Renee safe at home, miles away? But even in anguish that voice was familiar, a forlorn, desperately frightened wail, and unmistakably her voice.

Immediately as it was silenced another voice lifted, choking between rage and supplication, to be cut off in turn. About it also he found a familiar ring, which under the circumstances was not too surprising. It had been the voice of Robert, her brother. He could hardly be mistaken.

A desperate struggle was taking place as some of the boat's crew sought to silence those who had cried out, as they had taken advantage of the confusion from the near collision.

The long shadow of some ship other than the *Indefatigable* lay across the water, the boat at its edge. Overhead, the rising moon seemed to watch curiously. For an instant its light revealed a face, white and desperate, then a coat muffled it and any further outcry.

Taken with the voices, Hubbard had seen enough. Unmistakably Renee and her brother were in that boat, clearly made captive much as he had been, held against their will.

Along the Connecticut shore Bran Hubbard had a reputation for Yankee caution. With it was a matching trait, that, having surveyed a situation and reached a conclusion, he would go headlong to hell to carry it out. He had been concerned to remain unobserved, to keep out of trouble. Now a swift stroke brought him alongside the boat, then he grasped it near the gunwale. The other small craft was drawing away, its crew still muttering recriminations. A confused mass writhed and struggled, attention fully occupied.

The boat rocked as Hubbard hoisted himself aboard. With the cessation of rowing it had drifted deeper into the shadow. He made out a uniform, the officer with a sword in scabbard. Balancing on his knees, Hubbard came erect. An oarsman looked up, startled, as Hubbard's hand rested briefly on his shoulder, leaning to extract the blade.

Its weight and balance were reassuring. He had expected no better than a dress sword, a going-ashore article for adornment, but this was a long-bladed weapon intended for offence. Clearly the crew from this boat had been engaged ashore in as grim a business as that of the press gangs.

Sensing his loss, the officer swung, then checked as he found the point of the blade at his throat. Errant moonlight showed the rising red of anger in his cheeks, wiped away as by a stroke.

The still confused huddle did nothing for vision, but Hubbard made out that there were at least two women aboard, closely held, half smothered in the coats thrown over them.

"Be easy, now," Hubbard cautioned, as a man turned in swift amaze. Blankness replaced any thought of resistance in other faces. What ship these might be from remained to be discovered, but Hubbard wanted none of any of those lying in this harbor on this particular night. For Renee and her brother the shore would be better, hardly less for himself.

"Head –" he began, then further words choked on his tongue. As had been the case on the farm during the afternoon, the unseen and not to be guarded against had come from behind. A heavier darkness was closing, much as the waters had done so a short while before.

In his awakening there was a hauntingly familiar quality combined with the unreal, as though he had known it all before, even to the same sensations. A dull ache seemed planted deep inside his skull, like the rasp of saw and hammer in the Poynter shipyards. He'd been called hard-headed, and apparently that had saved him from a broken skull.

With increasing awareness he sensed the familiar motion of a ship, complete with sounds and smells – apparently the easy wash of waves in harbor, rather than breasted to the drive of wind in the sails. But a ship unmistakably. Painfully he screwed open his eyes, striving to recall at the point where memory had suddenly ended –

He'd been in the boat, assuming command, about to order them to pull for the shore –

Beyond that was only blankness. Yet there had been no one in the boat behind him, to catch him off-guard. Still it had happened.

Except that he was alive, which under the circumstances was rather more than might have been expected, the situation was hardly promising. But his own troubles concerned him less than did Renee's. She had cried out that she was being abducted.

Sitting erect increased the ache inside his skull, but at least he was not tied. Which suggested that he must have been unconscious for quite a while, a supposition reinforced by the dryness of his clothes. They had been dripping when he'd pulled himself into the boat. Then it had been evening, and now it was day. Further inspection assured him that he was in a small cabin, rather than stowed away in the forecastle or dark hole.

A step warned him of company. Turning

his head, he found Denny Poynter looking down.

THIRTEEN

Poynter was smiling, the oblique look of a cat holding a mouse in its claws. The long months since the *Red Savage* and the *Lively Lady* had put to sea had worked little outward change. Darkly, almost sleekly handsome, had he been a cat he would have purred. Never the possessor of a poker face, triumph and malice were blended.

"You're a hard-head devil, Hubbard." His voice was casual. "My bos'n broke his oar against your skull, as we came up behind, and it would seem that the oar suffered most."

The pieces were falling into place. Explained was not only what had happened to him, but Renee's abduction, probably tricked along with her brother. Arriving at the home of the Marquis, Poynter had been already informed of the state of affairs, not only as they concerned Captain Sir Harry Dupont, but that Hubbard was alive and ashore as well. From that situation, presented with an opportunity, it was not surprising that

Poynter had moved swiftly to avail himself of so unexpected a chance.

In the context of abduction, he was moving with his customary blend of recklessness and caution, himself an inheritor of the Yankee tradition. At times daring to an extreme, he had kept aloof while in the town and harbor, trusting the necessary chores to picked men from his crew. Even after reaching the town, he had engaged a separate boat, shadowing the others on their way to his ship, which of course would be the *Lively Lady*.

The caution which tempered his recklessness showed in that. Should anything go amiss on English soil, he preferred to watch from a distance, to disclaim responsibility. But his boat had kept close enough for intervention at a critical moment.

Poynter helped himself to a seat. He proffered no apologies or regrets for so murderous an attack.

"You always have had the damnedest way of turning up, just when no one would ever look for you," he complained. "I had supposed that you would of course have gone to the bottom along with the *Red Savage*. That would have been a fitting and gallant end for a fellow-townsman."

"Gallant, perhaps, for the rest of the poor fellows aboard her, but hardly fitting."

Poynter shrugged.

"Perhaps you're right. The whole affair was unfortunate, a result which you can understand was not intended. The *Red Savage* was much too valuable to sacrifice needlessly."

Such a hit had been the fortunes of war. Neither bothered to pursue it.

"I take it that you were the chief cause of the excitement in and around the Britisher," Poynter went on. "An interesting chain of events, to escape going down with the *Savage*, reach the shore, then be swept up by a press gang, escape them, and finally to stumble into my affairs. As my father used to put it, the devil looks after his own."

He was clearly in an introspective mood, impressed in spite of himself by the destiny which seemed to thrust a ribald finger into their affairs.

"It's curious, how the three of us have always been involved – Renee, and you; and me. If I'd been superstitious, I'd have given up, long ago, and left the field to you. Which would have been a mistake, for now the luck runs my way." He stood, abruptly.

"After that clout with the oar, you were lying in the bottom of the boat, apparently dead. So they hoisted you aboard. *I'd* have

94

dumped you over the side. Maybe it's better, this way."

He shrugged and departed, his words a not too subtle reminder that Hubbard could still be turned over to Dupont, to suffer the punishment prescribed for such an attempt at desertion. Hubbard was not only in Poynter's hands, but even a successful scramble from the frying pan would plunge him into the fire.

The recollection that another and even more pleasurable interview awaited him actuated Poynter to so abrupt a leave-taking. It was a meeting to which he had long looked forward, as triumphant as in his boldest dreams. His resolution had remained as unaltered through the years as his boyish promise that he would find Renee and carry her off as his prize.

Now, not merely a prize, but at need, a hostage.

That he sailed increasingly stormy seas was uncomfortably apparent. Along the way, almost imperceptibly, his luck had turned, betraying him. It had begun when the twin privateers had escaped from the Sound on that night of storm, only to encounter the British ships in what threatened to be a duel to the death. He'd fully intended to play a part –

Then had come the wild impulse to leave the *Red Savage* and Hubbard to what seemed certain destruction, to be rid of such a rival once and for all. A mad notion, rendered impossible of reversal after the *Savage* had incredibly turned the tables on its adversaries –

Leaving him branded coward and traitor –

A week later, luck had laughed anew, when in the confusion of night and storm he'd attacked what he took to be a British merchantman, to discover too late that it was American, and sinking under his feet – but not before a handful of survivors had gotten away in a small boat, to carry a tale of infamy –

His mood increasingly savage, impatient of the number and value of ships available for prey, he had swung all the way; since he had the name, he might as well have the game. It had been far simpler to rob and sink the very ships which he had set out to protect, to become, in the eyes of all, nothing less than a pirate.

Freebooting had paid handsomely, and of late there had been an added dividend – his acceptance by the British as an ally, their protection as he approached the shore of England. They too, might regard him as a pirate, a turncoat to be despised, but, hard-pressed anew by the return of the Corsican, they tolerated him. War, no less than politics, made for strange bedfellows.

His plan for the afternoon had been similar to Hubbard's – to find Renee, pay his respects, and discover if a dream was only that, or if it contained reality. Such a visit should be a pleasant interlude.

To be able to tell Renee that he was working for her and her father's cause, not against them – that, he had hoped, would please them, proving an open sesame.

Sight of her had affected him much as it had done with Hubbard. The dream *was* reality.

The news that she was promised to an English sea captain had shaken him. That this captain was commander of the big frigate anchored not far from his own *Lively Lady* had increased his rage and apprehension.

The additional discovery, that Hubbard had been there, the virtual certainty that Renee had favored Hubbard above the Englishman – and beyond question, above himself, had shaken and enraged him. Again, he had acted on impulse.

Masking his eagerness, proposing a course of action to Renee which her parents had found acceptable, he'd lured her away, not only from them but from Sir Harry and the British navy.

It was a heady triumph, tempered by the

97

realization that he had sacrificed his hard-bought favor, the protection of the British navy. Now, if they suspected the truth, they'd turn to hunting him down, bend every effort to his destruction.

It was not amiss, under such circumstances, to have an additional hostage.

Delayed reports, that the rumor of Napoleon having escaped, contradicted their wildness. Which left his own situation more dubious than before, even while they might prove portents of things to come.

FOURTEEN

Always a gambler, and possessing such hostages, holding what he counted as high cards, Poynter was in excellent mood as he knocked on the door of the cabin assigned to Renee. Her maid, as he'd contrived before she had set out for town, was with her. Such small courtesies were easy to afford and should make a difference in her ultimate attitude.

Engaged with getting the *Lively Lady* under way and out from a harbor aswarm with ships which would turn hostile if they had an inkling of what was going on, he'd had no time while the night lasted for anything else. Only with a freshening wind to give the *Lady* that liveliness for which she was famous had he drawn a full breath.

Now they were well away from the English shore, out from the harbor, beyond the Devil's Point. Plymouth was no longer even a speck on the horizon. And while they might encounter British ships on patrol at any time, they would not be aware of any change in the status of the *Lively Lady*.

That, however, might come at any moment. This cutting-out operation had been timed to a sword's edge. Sir Harry had returned to his ship in a towering rage, not quite understanding all that had transpired, but determined to discover what had gone amiss.

By now, he might well have done so. There could be turmoil both on shore and on the sea. He might well be in pursuit, determined alike on a rescue of his lady and vengeance on so infamous a pirate as the infamous Yankee was proving.

But for the moment the wind was sending the *Lady* along at a clip which no frigate could hope to match, and there were open seas ahead. Calling a warning of his intention, Poynter thrust open the door.

Renee, white-faced, swung to front him. To his surprise, eyes or face showed no ravages of tears. A woman grown, she was still the slip of a girl who had clung so stubbornly in his memory, even more beautiful than that memory had pictured.

Her maid, as youthful but fashioned along the lines of a dreadnaught, which would show more formidably with the years, emitted a small shriek. For all their plight, Renee had commanded, and she was engaged about her lady's hair-do – something already so exquisite and intricate as to be beyond the comprehension of any mere man.

Renee's brother, Robert, had been staring morosely from the small round window of the cabin. He turned with equal abruptness, his face patrician rather than handsome, nostrils pinching. Poynter recalled that neither he nor Hubbard had liked him as a playmate. For Renee's sake they had tolerated him.

Clearly he was minded to speak, but neither had any time for him. Renee was recalling that he had counseled and encouraged Poynter's suggestion of a journey to Plymouth. She was the quicker.

"Beast!" she flung at Poynter, the single word, but a hundred could have said no more.

Poynter had planned an entirely different approach. In the heat of such fire his good resolutions melted like wax.

"You change your tune over-readily," he

reminded. "Yesterday you were eager for my help, all but imploring me to save you from the fate intended for you by your father and future husband."

Renee's face had been pale. Now it flamed, whether from shame or anger, Poynter was at a loss to judge. His words were a deliberate affront, based on what he had sensed, but certainly unspoken.

Robert succeeded in having his say.

"As I've pointed out, you behaved not only too hastily but like a shameless hoyden. Even my effort to assure you protection, to save you from the fruits of such folly –" he threw up both hands disparagingly. Poynter noticed that his fingers glittered with rings, set with costly stones. Not for Robert d'Ernee the hardships of war and impoverished peoples.

Renee flashed him no more than a glance. She could have reminded him that he had insisted on his role, to no profit when she had needed assistance, only to his own discomfiture. Still, he had proffered, and however unwelcome his reasons, she gave him a measure of credit.

"I remembered you as a neighbor, with pretensions even beyond friendship, and you expressed a desire to be of help," she stormed at Poynter. "At least you told the truth as regarded Sir Harry Dupont and the activities of his crew, and I understood your allusion to Bran Hubbard's peril –"

She broke off, burying her face in her hands, conscious of its revealing wave of scarlet. Robert had been only too right, she had behaved like a credulous fool, however encouraged by her parents and himself. Poynter's promise of escort and protection to the town and back, his possible intervention on behalf of a common boy-and-girl friend –

Poynter hid a smile. That had been genius on his part, impelled by memory of an always hated rival, the friendliness even affection, which this strange contradiction of a woman had never hesitated to show where Hubbard was concerned. He had choked down a renewed fury of jealousy when the bait had worked, overridden by the satisfaction that Hubbard must be beyond help.

That Hubbard had managed to escape the clutches of the press gang, even after being taken aboard the *Indefatigable,* to evade capture and seize command of his own boat, with Renee in it –

Poynter shrugged. Almost he had succeeded in the rescue. Only his own fox-like lurking had fortuitously turned the tables. Now his luck ran strong, and he was master of it as he was master aboard the *Lively Lady.*

"You should count it a mercy that Hubbard was faring better than I had supposed possible. For what I did I had expected some measure of gratitude."

"Gratitude?" Renee flashed. "For abducting me? I see it all, now – how you made the most of circumstances, lying with just a veneer of truth to render your story plausible. You planned it from the first. Having known you, I should have understood."

Poynter had planned to deny everything, to insist that he had staged a charade only to avoid worse, given the confusion attendant in city and harbor. That, he realized, was useless, and after all, it did not matter.

"I made you a promise, back in Connecticut," he reminded now. "To come and carry you off at our next encounter. You perceive that I keep my word."

His boastfulness had not moderated with the years. His ready acceptance of all charges staggered her.

"You admit it, then? So monstrous an act? Right under the noses of – of everyone!"

"Was it not magnificent?" he countered. "Something that no one could have foreseen, therefore not to be guarded against. It has ever been my way, to move boldly. And for you, of course, most of all."

103

Renee's recovery was swift. Even as a girl she had always outmatched him.

"It is true, you have built a reputation," she acknowledged. "I have heard tales, even here in England – reports of a turncoat, a man traitor to his own land and cause, a privateer turned pirate! Now you confirm them, with the destruction of the *Red Savage*, of your fellow-countrymen, even your own townsmen –"

She broke off, her face going from angry pink to a strained white.

"What of Bran? Of Mr. Hubbard, whom you struck down as he tried to come to our aid? What have you done with him?"

"To the devil with him! He's safe enough – and right where I want him!" Poynter's fury exploded. Renee's words and manner were alike revealing. He was compelled to the realization that nothing had changed with the years. Even as a girl she had loved Bransom Hubbard, and after his gallant attempt at rescue, it was even more apparent. Poynter's hope to show well in her eyes had produced an opposite effect.

"You don't seem to understand," he went on blindly. "I've risked everything to reach England, to visit you, then to bring you here. What I said or did had nothing to do with Hubbard's welfare or this English captain,

104

only with you! I've wanted you since the first day I set eyes on you! I told you, over and over again, that one day I'd have you – and now I do!"

He watched her shrink back with increasing realization of the situation, of her own plight. After so many rebuffs, triumph was a tasty morsel.

"And since you don't seem inclined to show a proper appreciation, there's nothing to prevent me from taking it!"

His weakness had always been that he could play a role only to a certain point. When a course became irksome his true nature had a way of asserting itself. And be damned to consequences.

He moved suddenly, thrusting her maid aside with a lunging shoulder, snatching Renee in his arms before she could evade his rush. A savage lift of his boot caught Robert in the stomach as he strove to aid his sister, flinging him back across the room, to lie retching and gasping. Renee's frantically clawing hands he confined in one of his own, with a ruthlessness which brought sudden fear to her eyes.

FIFTEEN

Finding a desperate reserve of strength, Renee tore one hand loose and slapped him across the mouth. His lips caught against teeth which snarled rather than grinned, and the ferocity became real as they showed blooded from the impact. The saltiness spurred him, then he jerked his head about, incredulous with fury, at the dragging clutch of fingers on his arm, twisting him away, pulling him as helplessly as though he had been a rag doll.

Hubbard's face matched his own for fury. He had followed more slowly, legs faltering and uncertain, but the door to the cabin, imperfectly latched, had swung partly open, allowing him to hear and see.

He was unconscious of intent, only of acting, the weakness gone in the rush of hate. Recovering, Poynter lashed out wildly, missing, and Hubbard struck in turn, his knuckles working fresh outrage against the already lacerated lips and teeth. Poynter bawled wildly for help, but he did not attempt to regain his feet.

At least a dozen men, officers and sailors, responded, spilling through the door, swarming over Hubbard. There was nowhere to go, and they were too many for arms as suddenly drained of strength as anger had stimulated them.

Poynter's usual urbanity had gone the way of his dignity. On his feet, he glared about, tongue caressing battered lips, the whiteness about his mouth where Renee had slapped giving way to a returning flood of angry color. A second time he tasted, as though finding savor in the blood.

Repression was more terrible than the sudden vent to his rage. To have been bested, first by a woman, then by Hubbard, was bad enough. That his humiliation had been witnessed was insufferable. His barked order was more yelp than snarl.

"String him from the yardarm!" He emphasized the sentence with pointed addition. "Now!"

The clutching fingers on Hubbard's arms tightened, but beyond that, none of his captors moved to drag him away. Poynter was captain, the *Lively Lady* his ship. And like it or not, they were his crew.

They had responded with varying degrees of willingness to orders not always to their liking, but which to refuse would be mutiny. Most had come to accept with a growing hopelessness, a realization that he had dragged them along with him to a point beyond return. Memories of high hopes had been overlain by ashes.

But some of them had known Bran Hubbard, and old liking was strengthened by a fresh respect. One officer found courage to protest.

"Is no that a bit drastic, Captain? And himsel' like the rest of us, from the Connecticut shore –"

"A shore to which we'll never return, thanks to the likes of him," Poynter reminded. "He's a risk to all our necks. You'll carry out my orders, Mr. Sullivan."

Renee had shrunk away, white-faced, listening with a mounting incredulity. Now she protested in turn. "But you can't! It's murder!"

Poynter had control of himself again, but his temper was only in leash. His bow held sardonic mockery.

"Then murder it'll be. And on this ship I can do whatever I please, Madam. Ye'll do well to keep it in mind."

Those of Poynter's crew looked grim. Most of them had embarked on a voyage of indefinite duration and questionable success, impelled partly by the richness of prizes to be taken, but also by a sense of patriotism to their hard-pressed country. Poynter had led them far astray from those intentions, placing them in a double jeopardy before they fairly sensed what he was about. A noose of events drawing ever tighter, until it had become impossible to turn back.

For that reason they kept on with Poynter, since whatever safety remained was with him. But this order overstepped all bounds. Hubbard was a fellow Yankee, from Connecticut.

Opposed to their strong dislike for Poynter's capricious behavior was the awareness that at sea a captain held the powers of life and death, and mutiny was reason enough for the latter. It crossed Hubbard's mind that Mad Josh had not been the only shipmaster touched by the eerie.

A fresh twist of wind, erupting like a blowing whale out of a calm sea, rattled their sails, setting the *Lively Lady* aback. It was followed by more, the horizon drawn in as by a giant hand, tempest striking swift and hard. At this season of year such manifestations were to be expected, though usually with more warning.

Poynter was bawling fresh orders, his momentary purpose forgotten in the greater emergency. Hubbard was sent scrambling with the rest to take in sail, to batten down. The rain came as he worked, a drenching deluge. One man was swept away, plummeting far out, to be swallowed in the thickening gloom, the wild despair of his cry cut short.

For two days and nights the gale gave them no respite, driving them westward. Thanks as much to an efficient crew as a sturdy ship, they weathered it with no great harm, but all else remained in abeyance. Then the exhausted crew were able to stumble below and fall into exhausted sleep. Only Robert d'Ernee and his man had been spared the ordeal.

And even though he was still alive, Hubbard reflected, he'd had no further chance of a word with Renee.

He awoke to mess call, a hot meal finally prepared after nearly seventy hours on cold snacks, but to cook under such conditions had been impossible. Stiff and bleary-eyed, unshaven, he ate hungrily with the rest, then, unheeded, ascended the deck. Long rollers still moved under a sunlit sky.

A hail came from the lookout as he came into the open, more a startled interjection than a warning. Renee and her brother were on deck ahead of him, Renee as fresh as though there had been no storm, Robert showing haggard though freshly shaven.

Poynter stumbled up from below, bearded alike, clearly having been catching up on missed sleep. Half asleep on watch, the lookout had permitted a strange sail to approach dangerously close and unobserved.

Poynter cursed, in his voice a sudden panic. The *Lively Lady* was coasting comfortably, but under no more than half the canvas which the newcomer showed. That he had slept overlong, when he should have been alert and on his quarter-deck, and so was partly responsible for the surprise, made it no better. He berated the lookout for carelessness, but his own had allowed them to be tricked into a risky if not precarious position.

The newcomer was bearing down, with the clear purpose of intercepting them. What that might mean was to be discovered, but in times such as these a prudent captain always feared the worst. A friendly flag might seek only an exchange of news, after weeks or months of going with no recent reports as to how the world waged or war was waged. Now and again one would have a message of importance to all others.

At least as likely, any strange sail might prove an enemy, as eager for a prize as the *Lively Lady* had showed herself on numerous occasions when the odds not alone of surprise

111

but with weight of armament had lain with her. The attitude of this strange sail suggested that those odds were now in her favor and that she knew it and was prepared to make the most of them.

Hubbard, surveyed the newcomer with appraising eyes. Renee, accompanied by her brother, watched as well, from half across the deck. Robert's face was haggard with strain, white with nameless apprehension. But color rode like flags in Renee's cheeks, her eyes alive.

By her lines, the sprightly grace with which she cut through the water, or seemed almost to dance above it, here was another American privateer, longer, larger, heavier gunned than themselves. For the moment Hubbard could find no sure points of recognition, but that might soon be remedied. The gap was closing. Poynter, caught napping, was already in a bind, should the newcomer prove hostile. It was too late to crowd on sail, to hope to make a race of it.

Poynter, well aware of his own ship's capabilities, had reached the same conclusion. At best, considering the speed of the stranger's approach, the *Lady* would be lively enough to no more than hold her own. Left scant room in which to run or maneuver, she would be overhauled as she sought to swing, to take full advantage of the wind.

On even terms he might have risked the try. Only these were uneven, and growing more so. A circumstance which clearly accounted for the other's easy confidence. Some points to the west, but showing larger by the moment, a second ship was converging.

Here was the luck of the sea, the always present possibility of swift change or possible disaster. The difference was that the one captain, though weathering the same storm, had remained alert. What ensued now would depend, at least in part, on his intentions, as well as on what response Poynter might make.

His voice rising on an ill-suppressed note of panic, Poynter gave orders for a normal readiness, crews hastening to man the guns. But the washed-out look of his face, under the shadowing beard, testified to his apprehension.

The second ship was looming larger. Only then, like taunt or afterthought, did the first show her colors, and a muffled gasp which was almost a cheer went up from the *Lady*'s tensely watching crew. Hubbard swallowed around a sudden lump in his throat. He'd guessed right, studying the lines

113

of the newcomer, but never had the stars and stripes of his sorely tried nation appeared more beautiful.

In the event of action against odds, Hubbard did not trust Poynter, since the captain clearly did not trust himself. His conquests had come through surprise and treachery.

Poynter now was instant in response, the flag which he had desecrated and hauled down soaring aloft in matching greeting.

Glancing across to where Renee watched, Hubbard caught her sudden dazzling smile.

Poynter passed a handkerchief across his face. Color was replacing the pallor of his cheeks. Then his hopefulness was disturbed by the cautious remark of Mr. Sullivan, followed an instant later by a still more suspicious gesture from the approaching ship.

"There's a strangeness about her, sir — something not quite right. American she may have been built, but I misdoubt that she's American now —"

As though to confirm his opinion, the stars and stripes came down. In its place a fresh pennant soared, rare enough in these waters to be in itself a question-mark.

114

Poynter's jaw sagged between bewilderment and doubt.

"Dutch!" he ejaculated. "But what sort of a game is she playing? I don't like this."

"No more do I," Sullivan concurred. "'Tis as though he tricked us into showing our colors, but finds them less than pleasing. It's as though he thought to recognize us, but is not too certain."

The moldy bread which Poynter had cast upon wild waters appeared in a fair way to be returned.

SIXTEEN

Sullivan's guess could be all too accurate, considering the hide and seek game which Poynter had played for months, working to deliberately confuse the identities of the *Red Savage* and the *Lively Lady*. At the time he had found it pleasantly amusing, a convenient cover for treachery as well as a blow both at his country and at Hubbard. All at once, the web was in danger of tangling its weaver.

The distance between was steadily narrowing. Hubbard, possessed of a sharper pair of eyes than most, made out the name on the approaching ship, as clearly Dutch as her flag. *Wilhelmina.*

That her master was driven by more than simple curiosity, and that he also meant business, was indicated by matching activity aboard his vessel. A bank of guns had been run out in preparation for instant action, a move sufficiently strange following identification, since the Dutch and American forces were not hostile. And those guns, frowningly displayed, were grimly impressive. Hubbard judged the *Wilhelmina*'s armament at almost double their own.

Poynter took his decision, his face again colorless under the sharp glare of sun. He shouted orders for Renee and her brother and Hubbard to be hustled out of sight, ducking as promptly from view as well.

"Below with them," he added urgently. "You'll speak to him, Mr. Sullivan – answer as your wit dictates. We'll fight if we must, but he'd be a madman to fire on an American ship. Perhaps he's just suspicious."

Of that there was no room for doubt. The second ship held its course, and the figures aboard the Dutchman were fast becoming distinguishable. A hail came, from lungs accustomed to shouting against a gale.

"What ship is that?"

Hubbard, overhearing, was surprised, and

he darted a glance at their bows before being hustled out of sight. During his time aboard, with the stresses of storm, he had been much too busy to pay attention to such details, nor curious concerning them. The name on the *Wilhelmina* was plain and clear to read. But though the eager figurehead of the *Lively Lady* jutted from their own bow, the name had vanished. It could only have been painted over, and the blank space where it had been was reason enough for suspicion.

Sullivan was prompt with his reply. Clearly he possessed both the wit and the nerve for so ticklish a situation.

"*Red Savage*, Connecticut built." Coolly he added, "Captain Hubbard commanding."

From the gloom of the 'tween-decks Hubbard heard the click of Poynter's jaws, but apparently he was not displeased. Then he was gone, driven by urgency. Hubbard could no longer see, but the voices were clear.

"Who are you?" Sullivan challenged in turn, and that was the right note, bold and irritated. "Will you tell me what this is all about?"

Though civil in turn, the reply still couched on a note of anger.

"Captain Van der Kuylen, and we show our name." His English was heavily accented. "*You* should know what it's about – showing

117

no name which, taken with reports of piracy, makes certain ships as much a stink as a mystery."

"So! Now you become clear. This is the *Red Savage,* but no traitor or pirate. Still your wonder is reasonable, since it was the *Lively Lady* which was both, attributing her own deviltry to us as a blind. Which she will do no longer."

"How, sir? What will be your meaning?"

"She lies at sea bottom, somewhere off the English coast from Plymouth – and sent there by the *Red Savage.* Who else?"

If true, that must be accounted excellent news as well as a fair explanation. But Van der Kuylen's next question, while natural, promised to be less easy to answer. Yet on the reply their survival might hinge.

"If such is the case, where then is your captain? Let me speak with Hubbard. I've a man here who knows him." Apparently in proof, the sailor beside him was prompting urgently. "And for the matter of that, what about Captain Henderson? Mad Josh? He was Master."

Hubbard strained his ears for Sullivan's answer. Flanked by four guards, two of whom flourished belaying pins, while a third clutched a leveled pistol, he could not rush to the deck to show himself; in any case the

118

wisdom of such a course would be doubtful. But Captain Van der Kuylen's doubt was clearly mounting.

However much he might be sweating, Sullivan was playing his part to the hilt. He answered without hesitation.

"Captain Henderson was killed in the engagement against the *Lively Lady*. As for Captain Hubbard, he's asleep, after forty hours without closing his eyes, during the blow we've just come through."

That was a reasonable excuse for the captain's tardiness in appearing, but at best it could purchase only a little time. Van der Kuylen was clearly not the man to be put off with excuses.

That Denny Poynter had recognized that certainty from the first and was desperately playing for time, for a means to persuade Hubbard to cooperate, became clear as he reappeared, ordering Hubbard to follow. With the guards still in a tight cluster around him, obeying the command was academic.

Hubbard staggered as the *Lively Lady* heeled suddenly, laying far over. The roar of wind blasting through rigging and tortured sails smothered all lesser sounds. Then it was over with almost as swiftly as it had struck, no more than an errant gust, but too abrupt to be guarded against. But its effect on a ship with widespread sails could approach the disastrous. While the *Lively Lady* leaped like a bucking horse, the *Wilhelmina* would be having similar problems. There was a scurry of wildly running feet as men strove to restore order, to bring the still pitching vessel under control.

By itself, the interruption was of no great importance. But it could afford Poynter a desperately needed respite, sending the two ships farther apart – time for whatever he might be planning.

That his ship was in deadly danger was manifest, and for a few frantic moments he had seen no chance for a counter-play. At best, Sullivan could play no more than a delaying game, and Van der Kuylen's call for Hubbard could not be disregarded. The rub was that Hubbard had no reason for playing Poynter's game. If allowed to speak with Van der Kuylen, he might blurt out the truth and ask for assistance.

Then, suddenly inspired, Poynter had issued orders, and these had been executed.

Poynter rejoined Hubbard. Renee was a few paces to one side, also under watch.

"If you and Renee will come with me – oh, for only a moment, and so that there may be no misunderstanding." His tone was sardonic. "As you will appreciate, the welfare

120

of everyone depends on the reply we furnish – and especially is that true of your brother, Renee. Should anything go amiss, we will be forced into action. It would be most unfortunate should harm come to him."

Renee looked about wildly as Poynter led the way into the gloom of the 'tween-decks, doubly dark after the brightness of sun on water. The accumulated odors of foul air, cordage, men, tar, spun yarn and other things incidental to such a ship smote rankly.

Here was the ward room, spacious by the standards of most ships. In it, looming like shadowy monsters, three stern-chasers were in position, armament in addition to her broadsides. They were loaded and ready, though with muzzles not yet thrust out through the opened ports.

Though by themselves offering no particular threat to such a vessel as the *Wilhelmina*, the guns showed formidably. In conjunction with a broadside from the *Lively Lady*, they could fling an uncomfortable weight of ball and shrapnel.

The darkness, for the moment, disclosed nothing more. Here at mid-ship the pitch and roll of the *Lively Lady* was barely noticeable. Then a man went forward, holding a lantern. Its glow was yellow against the dark and struggling daylight.

Robert was revealed. Whether he had struggled to such effect that his captors had found it necessary to rap him smartly across the skull, or for other reasons, he hung, not quite senseless, dazed and vacant of face.

A part of that was perhaps the result of his plight, as with returning consciousness he was able not only to perceive but appreciate his situation, even while barely able to struggle against it.

Bound hand and foot, he hung in his bonds, stretched across the mouth of the middle cannon. With arms and legs additionally lashed to the carriage at either side, he sagged limply, a pitiful object, eyes rolling, incapable of speech.

Should the stern-chaser be touched off, he would be the first victim of the ensuing battle, the manner of his death horrible to contemplate.

SEVENTEEN

Renee checked suddenly, eyes great in a suddenly bloodless face. Then she cried out, her wail tortured and strangled. Her effort to rush to her brother's side was checked by her guards.

Hubbard's attention, like her's, was for Robert. During such opportunities as had been permitted him for observation, he had noticed the change which had taken place in Robert d'Ernee in the progression from youth to manhood. A guest of sorts in a distant land, Robert as a boy had been eager and friendly, largely forgetting his heritage along with the native land which had been little more than a memory.

But half a score of years in England had refashioned him, largely to the mold of the English and to others of his own rank who like him were exiled from France; men – and women – to whom the slogans of liberty, equality and fraternity had been an ill-timed jest. And though these had become largely catchwords under Napoleon, largely forgotten, he like the others detested the philosophy they represented.

He had an acquired arrogance, an air which in the country Renee had seemed to resent almost as much as did Hubbard. Even so, Robert was her brother, and what she saw was as horrible as it was unbelievable. Again she tried to go to him, to be held struggling and not too gently. She swung furiously on Poynter.

"What are you doing? This – oh, it is impossible! Loose him at once."

Poynter made a sweeping bow, suave, almost urbane. Crisis or not, he was enjoying this triumph, savoring the moment. His earlier rage was gone, leaving a fringing amusement.

"I quite agree with you, it is impossible. But necessary. Whether your brother has the distinction of being the first casualty in a battle which, once begun, might cost all of us our lives, or if he is to suffer no more than a brief inconvenience, depends on our old friend and neighbor, Mr. Hubbard. It is for him to say."

He swung lazily, but his tone was urgent.

"You perceive our situation. This infernal fool aboard the *Wilhelmina* suspects us of being other than we seem. He demands proof of what he has been told. I fear that nothing less than to see and speak with you, as the *Red Savage*'s captain, will satisfy him. And we must lose no time in getting on deck and making that reply. Convince him that this is indeed the *Red Savage*, under your command, and so soon as he is satisfied, my Lady's dear brother will be freed from this distressing inconvenience.

"But should you, for any reason, fail – then you perceive what must be the consequences."

It was not a matter permitting of argument, even had there been time. Poynter was already heading upward, Hubbard permitted now to go ahead and unguarded. Renee was still watched, leaving Robert to hang in his bonds, the gun crew ready for instant action. She threw back a despairing glance, then looked imploringly at Hubbard.

"I'll do my best, of course," he reassured her.

"That's showing good sense," Poynter approved, but his relief was manifest. "Convince those fools, and that will go a long way toward atoning for past mistakes."

Hubbard's thoughts were grim. For Robert and his plight, serious as it was, he was not overly concerned. Realization of what awaited him should it come to battle had brought him to near-collapse. Under the circumstances, such fear did him no discredit. But had it been only Robert's life at stake, it might have been a cheap price for a way out.

But the rest of them would be in a situation almost as bad. Poynter, like a cornered wolf, would fight, but he was not a man to win victory from the jaws of disaster. While the *Wilhelmina* and her captain would account themselves as doing not only a patriotic but necessary deed in sinking a pirate craft with its gaggle of traitors.

125

For Renee's sake, he must connive with such a deception, work to make it succeed. He could not allow the alternative, not even though he would be accounted traitor and pirate in turn.

Her master had the *Wilhelmina* under control again, her guns fronting them in ominous warning. The torn sail was being replaced, as the *Wilhelmina* coasted within easy hailing distance, or recognition.

Moving briskly to the rail, Hubbard noted that the companion ship had closed the gap, and was near enough for action. If he was actually in command he'd have no better choice than was imposed upon him, though he was of an opinion that he'd have found a way to give battle before allowing such an impasse.

"Sorry to show you a discourtesy, Captain," he called. "Hubbard speaking."

The man alongside the Dutch captain supplied confirmation. Hubbard did not recognize him, but he had been known to most sailors along the Connecticut shore.

"That's Cap'n Hubbard, right enough, sir. No doubt about that."

Van der Kuylen nodded, but he was still only partly satisfied.

"Sorry to have troubled you, Captain. But you'll understand why. Even

your ship's behavior stirs suspicion."

Hubbard understood. The claim had been
made that the *Lively Lady* was at ocean
bottom, that this was the *Red Savage*. But his
belated appearance on deck, as her captain,
and despite a ready explanation, hardly rang
true. The very change in motion would waken
a shipmaster and bring him on deck in a
rush. That he would sleep through such an
exchange as had already taken place strained
credulity.

Nothing short of a gamble was likely to
dissipate Van der Kuylen's mounting distrust.
Hubbard took it.

"If you care to spare the time to come
aboard," he invited, "I'd be more than happy
to crack a bottle with you, Captain."

There was a moment of hesitation. Should
Van der Kuylen avail himself of the invitation,
the situation would still be touch and go. But
at worst he could be seized and held as a
hostage. What might follow then would be
equally chancy.

But the readiness of Hubbard's invitation
was disarming. Van der Kuylen was already
gesturing to his first officer to veer away.

"Sorry, Captain Hubbard, but since all is
well with you, I can spare no more time.
Sorry to hear about Mad Josh. We'll spread

127

the word as opportunity offers that the *Lively Lady* is no longer a problem."

"I will appreciate that, Captain. This confusion of identities has been troublesome."

"That is easy to understand. Good luck to you and the *Red Savage*."

That had been a squeaker, and it was almost certainly a foretaste of things to come. Sooner or later events must catch up with Poynter, beyond dodging or evasion. As he returned to the deck, the *Wilhelmina* was already hull-down on the horizon.

Poynter was not adverse to gambling, though he preferred to know that he held the trumps. He had been sweating, but he was pleased at Hubbard's success in retrieving the situation; though not to the extent of admitting his own error.

"Good work," he commended. "You have your uses." He gave the order for Robert d'Ernee to be freed from his uncomfortable position.

Renee said nothing, disinclined to thank Poynter where she was more in a mood to berate him. The soft shine in her eyes as she looked at Hubbard more than told her gratitude.

Hubbard's impulse, which he could not act upon, was to take her in his arms, to comfort her, and, great lady though she was, he knew

128

that she would turn to him as she had done when suffering childish hurts. But on board this ship which Poynter had named after her they could hardly afford even to speak to one another. Her plight, even more than his own, gave Hubbard increasing concern.

Poynter, always acting on impulse, had gradually woven a net which now was closing about them. Captain Sir Harry Dupont, bubbled as he had been, would unquestionably exert every effort to get to the bottom of that seemingly disconnected series of events, in which he had been made to appear so poorly. By now he would probably be at sea, and unless to do so might be in direct conflict with his orders, he would be questing eagerly for the *Lively Lady*, determined both on rescue and destruction.

Almost certainly he would fit events and pieces into an understandable whole. His chance of finding them, a single ship on a vast ocean, was remote. But in so unlikely an event, their plight would bc even worse than when confronted by the *Wilhelmina*.

Poynter was beginning to realize how he had overreached. His weakness, as his dour father had more than once pointed out, lay in rashness both of speech and action. For almost the first time he wondered what

Sharkey Poynter must think of him, as uncontestable proofs of his son's conduct filtered back. He really hadn't cared. There had never been any love lost between father and son.

But Sharkey Poynter, money-grubbing and dour, held a deep love for land and flag. If called to sit upon a jury, he'd vote to hang any traitor, even his own son.

Victory was only respite. Poynter glowered at Hubbard and Renee, a little part from each other, but eying in an understanding which went beyond words.

"You should be grateful to me for making it possible for you to meet again," Poynter mocked. "And having the pair of you as hostages may prove of considerable worth."

EIGHTEEN

Poynter's overriding weakness, aside from impulsiveness, was a tendency to yield to impulse, to change his mind. He had pursued a course too far ever to turn back, but having recognized that, he was intent to find some way, and what better than by coercion, through the possession of hostages?

As for what Hubbard or even Renee might

think, he was past caring. He held the whip hand. The seas were wide, and the *Lively Lady* could show her heels to most ships. At need, she was a fighting ship.

"You'll keep apart," he warned. "I'll not have you conspiring together. The treatment you'll receive – all three of you – depends on your behavior."

Robert d'Ernee, coldly angry after his ordeal, made a preemptory demand that Poynter put them ashore at the nearest possible port. To his surprise, Poynter was agreeable.

"Oh, by all means. Nothing could please me better. When such a port is reached, we will all go ashore, to find a man of the cloth, who will marry Renee and myself. With you, her brother, consenting and approving."

Robert choked, incredulous at such effrontery. "You can't for a moment suppose that she would marry you – or that I would give my consent under any circumstances –"

"I'm certain that you'll both be more than eager, as opposed to *no* ceremony – and one, even two less hostages remaining." His pronouncement was threat and promise.

Hubbard was sufficiently skilled as a seaman to read sun and stars, to check prevailing winds and chart more or less roughly the ship's course and apparent destination. That they were heading as directly for the Indies as Poynter could manage did not surprise him. As a course for such a ship it was not only prudent but feasible.

Among those islands where Columbus had searched in vain for the spicelands of the East, the great Brotherhood of the Coast had for most of the following centuries maintained a loose but effective alliance and confederation. They remained now a possible haven, the only one where Poynter might find sanctuary.

For those who sailed under the skull and crossbones, there had been an ebb and flow with the years; now, with war washing the farthest horizons, the flow exceeded the ebb. There would be other pirate ships among those channels, and, more importantly for Poynter, other piratical crews, should his own become revolted at his excesses.

Some of the greater islands, such as Cuba and the Main, owed allegiance to Spain; others remained, more or less loosely, the property of the crowns of England or France. Among their waterways, strange flags plied.

Hubbard could only bide his time, of which there was an abundance, thankful that a further crisis was not being precipitated. But the certainty that one could not be long delayed settled as oppressively as the increasing heat of the waters into which they sailed.

A factor which Poynter had all but overlooked was becoming a cause for concern. It was now necessary for the *Red Savage* to play the part of an authentic privateer. As such, they could attack vessels under the British flag, but the sea, all at once, remained disappointingly empty of such prey.

Three times, contrarily, they sighted Yankee merchant vessels which had a look of fatness, but to snap them up might prove too risky. And to send a captive vessel into even a friendly port, with a prize crew, would be out of the question. Wide as were the oceans, the tale of the *Lively Lady*'s piracy had outraced her. Under her new guise she must sail circumspectly.

From Poynter's point of view, obsessed with his personal plans, it was a good solution, but his crew were not so easily persuaded. They had come not only to understand but to regard askance this captain who had led them into treason and piracy, and who would readily sacrifice their necks for the security of his own. Attainted of high crimes, they were being denied the sole reason for remaining at sea, the profits to be derived from an impartial exercise of freebootery.

They complained. Poynter reassured them airily.

"I but await a proper opportunity. Once it shows its sails above the horizon – have I ever failed you?"

It made an easy assertion, but within an hour the lookout was shouting at a sail, and as they swung to pursue the same course it took on size and shape. The crew clamored for what beyond question would be a rich prize, and seemingly with little enough risk – another Dutchman, this time of considerable tonnage, her rounded bow low in the water.

To American eyes she was unmistakably of the Netherlands, corpulent, comfortable, constructed more for utility than for speed or sailing qualities. And precisely what he was in need of, Poynter decided after some hesitation. Since he and his crew were in this together, and must stay together, better to placate them, to hold their loyalty against later tests.

Preparations were made for attack, quietly but efficiently, as the two vessels continued to converge. Outwardly there was no show of hostility. The Dutch flag soared aloft, to be matched by the American. They would pass close, to exchange courtesies, along with reports of anything new which affected their world – news almost inevitably of Napoleon, of England, possibly even of America.

Overlooked for the first time in days in the bustle of preparation, Renee made her way to where Hubbard watched. She wasted no words.

"I'm afraid. This – somehow it's like the smell of the swamps when the wind sets right." Her nose wrinkled daintily. "A smell of trouble. Or am I unduly apprehensive, Bran? I never supposed I was a coward, but now –"

"You never were or could be, Renee. But your instincts are correct. We're getting ready to attack, without warning."

"But that's piracy," she protested. "I thought he'd given that up. It would undo everything he's been trying to correct."

"He has been forced to realize that he's already gone too far, that sooner or later retribution is sure to catch up. We've been holding as straight a course for the West Indies as can be managed, which tells its own story. Best retire to your cabin, Renee. It will be unpleasant up here."

"Then I want to watch," Renee insisted. "After all, it concerns me – and you and Robert as well. And what difference does it make – so long as he controls?"

He sensed her fear then, the apprehension which had been building toward terror with each lengthening mile of the voyage. Courage was no bulwark against promptings of mind and heart.

Again, almost overmasteringly, his impulse was to comfort, to reassure her that somehow all would be well, but to lie would make it worse. And all at once time had run out.

The Dutchman made the first move, one clearly planned to take them by surprise. Her colors came down with a rush, followed an instant later by the hoisting of a flag rarely seen or so openly acknowledged – the black flag of the Brotherhood, on it in staring contrast the grisly white of skull and bones.

Even that might not be an accurate representation of the ship or its true intentions. Hubbard's guess was that she might be British, disguised for just such a purpose, showing sudden teeth as the cover was flung aside and her guns run out. The two ships were almost abreast, and such trickery was nothing new in war; under the black flag it required no explanation.

In the *Red Savage*, as the name proclaimed, she thought to behold the same sort of prize, one easy for the taking, that Poynter looked for in turn. The abrupt show of force should persuade her victim to abject surrender.

Poynter clearly was not much surprised,

and certainly not intimidated. In action, as he had more than once demonstrated, he was formidable, with reckless courage. Before the pirate flag was half-way up, the port broadsides of the *Lively Lady*, bearing at direct range, thundered defiance, a full five seconds before those of the Dutchman's starboard could reply.

At point-blank range no particular skill was required. The *Lively Lady* staggered to the impact, while her rival swerved wildly under equal punishment. Spars were crashing, sails cascading in a disordered tangle, billowing smoke from both sets of guns drifting around and over, hiding the worst of the carnage. Wounded men were crying or screaming.

To Hubbard it was familiar, and he turned, determined to escort Renee to shelter whether or not she was willing, but she had disappeared. The Dutchman was yawing crazily, so that he guessed a lucky shot had crippled her steering. For the moment the advantage belonged to the *Lively Lady*.

Determined to pursue it, Poynter shouted orders to take her past, then swing back so as to bring her other guns to bear. Hubbard gave credit to the seamanship of the crew, a skill not surprising for men mostly from his own town.

Then it was Poynter who miscalculated, in the smother of smoke which drifted like fog above the Dutchman, an error easy to stumble in to but almost fatal. Either he failed to understand or take into account the havoc of her smashed steering, but her own captain did not. With no volition on his part, his vessel poised for a broadside from her unused guns, and then it crashed at them, and the *Lively Lady*, taken wholly by surprise, staggered as though fatally stricken.

If she was not it was due more to the stoutness of her construction than to the mishandling to which she had been subjected. Wreckage was everywhere, the worst the loss of her mainmast, so badly shot away that it came crashing instants later. Across decks suddenly red, confusion was rampant. The helmsman sagged above the wheel, struck by a fragment of shell or flying debris. The *Lady* was drifting dangerously in turn.

In another moment she would be under the Dutchman's guns for a third and probably finishing salvo. Jumping, Hubbard grabbed the wheel. Sullivan was bellowing orders, his face a mask of blood and smoke. Men with axes made a frenzied attack on the tangle of sail and wreckage, and a part of the hampering mass was chopped loose. Wind filled such fluttering rags as remained and gave steerageway. Hubbard swung her, and the big shells whistled ominously but a fraction later past their bow.

Night was closing, and the darkness was their salvation. Half-crippled in turn, the Dutchman had the better of it, but not by much. Then darkness blotted them from each others' view.

Only Sullivan had noticed Hubbard's part. He relieved him, and Hubbard looked about for Renee, finally concluding that she must have sought her cabin. The work of clearing away wreckage, of rigging a jury mast so that they might at least hobble, with other necessary repairs and caring for the injured, continued for most of the night. Somewhat after midnight they were on the move again, after the manner of a wounded animal crawling away to lick its wounds.

With dawn the sea showed empty. Faces were haggard. The work of cleaning, of burying the dead, went on. The strange encounter had been a bootless sort of contest.

It was not until mid-morning that Poynter, grim and raging at the condition of his ship, thought to wonder about his unwilling passengers, the d'Ernees. A messenger, dispatched to make inquiries, returned with a frightened look on his face.

"Her Ladyship's cabin is empty, sir.

There's no sign of her or her maid – or of her brother. Nothing of either of 'em."

NINETEEN

For the next hour, Poynter was almost a madman. A frantic search was made of the entire ship, all else put aside in his desperate effort to find Renee and her brother. Not until it was proved that they were no longer on board would he accept that they could have escaped. But the absence of a couple of sailors, along with Renee's maid and Robert's man-servant, forced him to a final acceptance.

The actual endeavor, under the cover of the darkness and ensuing confusion, had probably not been too difficult. The pair of crewmen who had enlisted, either for gold or an equal desire to be free of such a ship, could have provisioned and lowered a boat, one of which was missing.

In the full light of day there was no sign of it. Whether they had gotten clean away, encountered disaster in the rough seas, or perhaps been picked up by the Dutchman, could only be conjectured.

Not unexpectedly, Poynter fixed on

Hubbard as the prime mover in such an escape.

"I should hang you out of hand," he raved. "Of course you'd do anything to get her away from me –"

"Why, and so I would," Hubbard interrupted. "Only I didn't. If I'd had a hand in the matter, I'd have gone along with them."

Poynter was taken aback at so obvious a certainty. Sullivan intervened.

"Mr. Hubbard could have had nothing to do with it," he pointed out. "At about the time it must have happened he was saving us all from destruction by grabbing the tiller at a critical moment, then working the ship through the worst of it. He couldn't have found time or chance to aid them."

And despite the readiness with which he'd professed a desire to go along, doubt was strong in Hubbard that he would have provided such assistance even if asked. He understood the desperation which had driven them to so wild an expedient, Renee's fear of Poynter and his intentions. Even the unknown terrors of an open boat had seemed preferable.

But it was a counsel of desperation, undoubtedly the notion of Robert d'Ernee. Since the role forced upon him in the encounter with the *Wilhelmina,* he had been increasingly apprehensive.

141

Poynter's impulse was to cruise widely in an effort to find them, but the condition of the *Lady* made that impossible. Crippled, no longer lively, she was barely able to limp. Should an enemy chance along, they would fall an easy prey.

Poynter's original intention had become desperate necessity. They must reach the Indies, to find some remote island where they could lie hidden long enough to fell trees and fashion a new mainmast, emplace it, and otherwise restore the *Lively Lady* to a semblance of her former self. Lacking the equipment of a shipyard with necessary facilities, it would be a formidable undertaking, but there was no choice.

Hubbard had no doubt that it could be managed. Among the crew were skilled artisans from Sharkey Poynter's shipyards, men who understood each operation and could contrive levers and counter-weights to compensate for lack of tools, to edge a giant timber into place and hoist it, then anchor it securely.

But that would take time, weeks or even months, even with the opportunity to work unmolested. Until the refitting was complete, they would be largely at the mercy of any enemy who might chance upon them.

But that was the fortune of war – good

fortune, by comparison with what had so narrowly been averted. And since every member of the crew realized that their ultimate survival depended on getting the job done, there could be no question as to their willingness.

The weather turned pleasant, a steady breeze pushing them. The seas remained empty.

After the countering of that initial outburst, Poynter ignored Hubbard. He was increasingly silent and moody, leaving the handling of the ship largely to Sullivan, prowling his quarter-deck at all hours of the day or night, after the manner of a phantom. Men viewed him askance. The voyage upon which they had embarked with high hopes had been turned into a nightmare. That Poynter was encompassed with the rest of them afforded scant comfort.

Sullivan was not only a good officer but practical. He approached his aloof captain with suggestions, which Hubbard overheard.

"I've been thinking that our luck's not all bad. In the long run, much of this may be all to the good."

"And by what curious twist of reasoning do you arrive at such a conclusion, Mr. Sullivan?" Poynter demanded.

"We've been a long while at sea," Sullivan

143

reminded. "And our bottom's increasingly foul. We've no such turn of speed as at the beginning. Once we find our proper harbor, we can careen and scrape her clean, since there's plenty of manpower for that while others are cutting and trimming a tree for the mast. That will leave us as good as new, better off than before."

Apparently such a notion had not occurred to Poynter. He gave grudging approval.

"It sounds feasible – if we can find a proper island with a good harbor. Do you know the Indies, Sullivan? Is there a man aboard with more than a general familiarity with them? Apparently not. To find what we want purely by hunt and chance may be to stumble into more trouble."

"There are two, I believe, with a fair amount of knowledge. Mr. Hubbard is one. Stamford is the other."

Stamford was an ill-favored man who might well have skulked among the islands as one of a full-fledged crew of freebooters.

"You'd search far to find a more unpromising pair," Poynter growled. That he owed his ship and probably his life to Hubbard's quick action during the last engagement rankled. He resented such a debt, and that it might be still further increased was added bitterness.

144

"Hubbard's a Jonah," he added. "Ever since we tangled with him, out from Plymouth, our luck has been the devil's own."

Sullivan was of Irish blood, with the blend of three generations of Yankee spirit added. Like others of the crew, his temper had shortened with the gradual but steady worsening of their situation.

"I'll agree with you that there's a Jonah aboard. But it's not Mr. Hubbard. He's been our salvation, not our curse."

Poynter's face flamed at the implication, to be as suddenly washed of color.

"Why, you – you – those are mutinous words, Mr. Sullivan."

Sullivan shrugged.

"Plain they are, but not mutiny. If I or the crew had been of a mind for that, we could have taken the ship long ago, but to what purpose? You led us astray, along with yourself, and by the time we recognized the noose, our necks were in it. This is a time for plain speaking. But since we're all in it, we can't afford not to work together."

"You've been talking to Hubbard," Poynter charged thickly.

"Why, so I have," Sullivan agreed. "But not along such lines." He seemed to muse aloud. "The sea works strange pranks with a man's mind – at least with the minds of some. There was Mad Josh – and in the long watches of the night, strange fancies creep. Even the best of us, having feet of clay, are prone to error."

Poynter swallowed, recognizing the excuse proffered him for his own mistakes. It was an olive branch he was not inclined to accept, but neither did he reject it.

"If you and Hubbard between you can bring us to such an anchorage as we require, we'll all be in your debt," he said grudgingly, and stumped away below.

Sullivan stared after, his face bleak. Then it eased to a grin as he swung toward Hubbard.

"Bearding a lion – or a captain on his quarter-deck – is not so easy," he observed wryly. "But it was a time for plain speaking. You heard?"

"I heard."

"Can you guide us to what we require?"

"There are a lot of such islands, scattered here and there. With a bit of luck we'll find one."

"We're in your debt already. That will deepen it. Though I'm wondering if we might not do better to scuttle what remains of such a ship, take to such boats as remain, and make as good a start as may be, among the islands."

It was a tempting notion, offering perhaps the only way out for men attainted of treason and piracy. Yet few if any would seriously consider it, not while a fundamentally solid ship was beneath their feet. In any case, as Hubbard pointed out, it possessed a fatal flaw.

"Even if we wished, we could never manage while Poynter is alive."

Sullivan's smile was sardonic.

"But what is a bit of mutiny or murder, added to crimes for which any court – or mob – would already hang us out of hand?" he wondered.

Luck continued to favor them, as though repenting of the harshness with which it had already buffeted. They were tossed by an occasional squall, sharp gusts of wind and torrential downpours, gone almost as swiftly as they blew up. The seas, which for a while had sprouted hostile sails, remained empty until the dark loom of land grew against the horizon, and it became apparent to everyone that ahead were the Indies, that a haven might not be far distant.

Hubbard had been at pains to point out to Sullivan that his knowledge of the islands was general rather than particular. Stamford had been unhelpful, and Sullivan placed no trust in him. Once they entered the tortuous channels which wound among some of the islands Hubbard made sure that they felt their way with every precaution, taking frequent soundings. The lush beauty among which they sailed was an indication of rather than a guarantee against danger.

There were islands, many rising abruptly out of the sea, some heavily wooded. The fragrance of tropical flowers wafted to them like heavy perfume. Mountains lifted, many of the slopes green with timber. They glimpsed the sparkle of waterfalls, the snowy white of beaches. Most of these were uninhabited, and in that thought was comfort. In their present state of unpreparedness, to be alone was essential.

Here were the more northerly keys. They approached an island which appeared to be fashioned to their need. A second and larger inland was not far to the side. Rounding the headland, they found and crept along an island channel, to where a sheltered lagoon gave upon a secret bay, of no great size but ample. Anchor was dropped.

The basin in which they found themselves was roughly pear-shaped, narrowed at the neck where they had entered. At its side a small hill, partially wooded, inhospitably steep, reared as though in warning. The recesses of the island lifted to near mountains, leaving them well screened from any chance observation of a ship which might thread the channels between islands. A stream coursed down to the beach, exciting lively comment.

"Fresh, cold water – not stale and swimmin' with the Lord only knows what," one man observed. "Such water as feeds the Beaverkill, where as a boy I visited an uncle and swam and fished!"

"Or the Delaware!" another echoed wistfully. "Such trout as it holds! And the great eels which come up from the sea! That was the life! Why ever I left it for such as this –"

He left thought and hope unfinished, as they must go unfulfilled because of the taint put upon them through following Poynter. Some of the glances cast his way were dark with hate, but he was cheerfully unobservant, as pleased as any at the prospects of some weeks ashore.

From shipboard the land gave every evidence of a tropical paradise, the shrouding greenery making the sea seem distant. Turtles scuttled apprehensively as the anchor chain rattled. Palm and pimento formed a green wall at the farther rim of white sand.

The opposite side of the little bay was

enclosed by a rocky rampart, largely screened by foliage. Unlike the others, Hubbard's attention was mostly for the hill, then for the slopes farther in the distance. They should contain trees of a size and quality suitable for the masts and other needed repairs.

Poynter seemed stirred from the dark mood which had gripped him since the battle. He issued no orders, leaving the handling of the ship to Sullivan, who presumably had some notion of how it should be careened for scraping, then to go about the work of repairs. As son of Sharkey Poynter, owner of a great shipyard, Denny had disdained to work in those yards, but he realized that some of the men had a practical knowledge along such lines.

With mere rags of sails, hardly stirred by a fading wind, the *Lively Lady* had crept in, creating little disturbance. Rapt gaze on the shore, Poynter exclaimed,

"Footprints! And, by heaven, a woman's, from their size!"

Others rushed to look, the word potent to conjure up memories, as varied as the mind of each beholder. Caught in the quickening interest, Hubbard made them out, a single line of barefoot tracks, leading from the rim of jungle, down to the shore line, then back the way they had come. His quick eye caught sign which escaped the others, where the remnants of the outer tide, working their way inland through the tortuous channels they had followed, still exerted their force. The tide was building, close to cresting. Some of the prints were being inundated, smoothed away.

Clear evidence that whoever had made them had been there only a short while before; possibly frightened away by a glimpse of the oncoming *Lady*, poking her nose through the channel, the figurehead at her bows seeming to scan bay and headland with a matching eagerness.

Prints small and dainty enough, beyond doubt, to be those of a woman. "No doubt about it, there's a woman," Poynter added. "And I'll find her!"

His face was dark with excitement as he poised, measuring the depth of the water, clearly minded to jump and wade to shore. The glitter in his eyes matched the wildest which had ever troubled those of Mad Josh.

He was on the verge of jumping when a hail, sudden and peremptory, checked him, swinging every man about as though jerked by a string. It came from the height of rimrock opposite, with all the quality of a disembodied voice.

151

"Ahoy the ship! A word with your bally captain, if you please – before we sink you!"

TWENTY

Hubbard was first to make him out, a tall man at the crest opposite from the beach, half-sheltered by the trees through which he had pushed. Unlike Sir Harry Dupont, he was spare and lean, nostrils pinching thinly in an aristocratic face. Like Sir Harry, he wore the uniform of a ship captain of the royal navy.

"Stand easy," he continued in sharp warning. "I'd have a word with you. And should anyone be so ill-advised as to consider me in pistol-range, why, so I may be! But so are all the rest of you. Take a look."

At the short jerk of a hand, three other men rose up suddenly, two to one side, one on the other – sailors, but each clutching a long-barreled musket. Then, again so swiftly that it had the aspect of illusion, they had ducked back out of sight.

"You're all well targeted, whereas you'd have nothing at which to aim," the captain continued, his voice on a reasonable, almost conversational note. "Is it understood? Ye have a captain, no doubt?" he added testily.

Denny Poynter shook himself. It was doubtful if any sort of surprise had ever shocked him so badly.

"I'm the captain," he returned. "We'll hear you – but no tricks! We can fight."

His eyes were darting apprehensively, clearly uncertain if this might prove to be an ambush, a prelude to attack. Hubbard had already dismissed such a possibility. In the other man's laugh was a hint of contempt.

"No trickery, I promise – and the word of Vane-Templeton is good, even when given to pirates! I'm here merely to avoid unnecessary bloodletting, which could be to no purpose, least of all to you, trapped like the rat y'are! I'll take your surrender in the morning."

Surprise had unnerved Poynter, but he was not lacking in courage. For the moment he saw no imminent threat.

"You're as gusty as the winds which blow among these islands," he returned.

"But such winds can founder a ship," Vane-Templeton reminded. "It's well-met we are, your *Red Savage*, and my *Calypso*. You've been hardily dealt with, forced to seek a haven from which to make repairs. You overlooked us where we lay sheltered in a nook behind yonder island, watching while you crept in. Had you noticed, we might have been forced to knock you about a bit more, even to sink you if you were such fools as to resist."

He was thoroughly enjoying this moment of triumph. He gave a complacent twist to a pointed wisp of mustache.

"I'll concede that the elements favored you. You had the benefit of a breeze, while we lay becalmed. But in these latitudes there's always a wind at dawn, and with it, we'll sail in to you. We can maneuver, which you cannot. You might loose a broadside, but it would be your last. For then we'd be compelled to send you to the bottom. And with a bit of reflection, I'm sure you'll find no profit in such an end."

The opposite point of mustache received attention.

"So it's hopeful I am that daylight will find you in a reasonable mood. At that time I will accept your surrender."

He was gone as suddenly as he had appeared, stepping back and down. The officers and crew of the *Lively Lady* continued to stare as though bemused, not merely at the show, but at the grim implications of Vane-Templeton's demand. It was no exaggeration that they were in a trap, from which there could be no escape. Even if they could set sail comparable to what the *Calypso* could hoist, and find wind to retrace a path to the open sea, Vane-Templeton could be there to contest the passage.

With mainmast gone and the others no more than stumps, they were unable to maneuver, to get out from the haven which had been made a trap. Vane-Templeton seemed justified of his confidence.

There was a dazed look on Poynter's face, but Hubbard had a different reaction. To a man with nothing to lose, an added threat was without significance.

Before anyone could react he went overside in a long dive, not toward the beach but opposite, among the deepening waters which washed the rimrocks. A few easy strokes carried him to a break in the wall, shrouded with moss and brush. He climbed, aided by vines, finding possible footholds. It was equally testing but less perilous than a frantic ascent from deck to top-mast.

He gained the parapet where Vanc-Templeton had stood, and the opposite slope fell sharply to the sea, half a hundred feet below. The headland made a scant but effective breakwater, guarding the inlet behind which the *Lively Lady* sheltered.

A small boat from the *Calypso* had put its

captain ashore. His confidence had probably stemmed from recent explorations in and about these islands, affording him a certainty as to what he would find. A quarter of a mile away, the boat receded across waters so smooth that scarcely a ripple showed. The captain steered, his back to Hubbard. Then he turned to stare, and seeing Hubbard, waved jauntily.

The oarsmen had put him beyond good musket range, even had Hubbard possessed a weapon. Some two miles farther, huddling close to the protective cover of the second island, Hubbard made out the *Calypso*. Unmistakably a man o' war, she looked to be a match both in size and armament for the *Lively Lady*.

Having watched the limping progress of the *Lively Lady*, correctly estimating her search for a haven, Vane-Templeton had been content to let her reach that secluded harbor which could so readily be turned into a trap.

Already tasting triumph, he had been unable to wait and complete the surprise with the guns of *Calypso* to back him. He'd put off in the small boat like a boastful small boy, to voice both warning and demand.

A demand backed by what he accounted overwhelming force. He had not been bluffing.

"Only indiscreet," Hubbard reflected, and studied the surrounding seas, the mountains lifting from islands no longer friendly. Almost to a man, those aboard the *Lively Lady* watched him.

It had never occurred to Hubbard that legends might grow around him as they had done with Mad Josh, or latterly with Denny Poynter. Or that in Hubbard of the *Red Savage* they rested their plight or possible hope of salvation. To Poynter there was neither hope or expectation of a possible miracle, as Hubbard made his way back and was assisted aboard. The tropical heat of the afternoon was intense, and the swim had been refreshing.

But a drowning man will clutch at straws. "Well?" Poynter jerked the question.

Hubbard shrugged. His voice was expressionless.

"It's as he said. *Calypso* appears comparable in size and armament."

Poynter's hard-held restraint broke. Each moment of reflection, of pondering and assessing their situation, had rendered him more frantic. That they were here out of necessity, putting in to what had appeared a perfect haven, not only with his consent but at his orders, he chose to disregard.

"So, thanks to your guidance, we're

trapped! Caught with no chance either to fight or run! I'm not doubting that you had something of the sort in mind when bringing us to such a spot!"

Hubbard had expected the reaction. Though not lacking in courage, in a moment of crisis Denny Poynter had no gift for leadership.

"Is it any worse fate to be sunk here than in the open sea?" he wondered.

"So you did plan it! A treacherous revenge because you'd been bested in fair fight! By God, I'll see you kick from a tree, before we are destroyed in turn. Seize him," he added wildly.

No one moved. Peril compassed them, and Poynter, as was abundantly clear, was not the man to find a way out, if indeed any existed. Hubbard shrugged anew.

"At least, we can go down fighting, if it comes to that. Or had you overlooked that possibility?"

"Overlooked it? Go down fighting? To what end?" Poynter gestured to the far rim where they had entered, where, shrouded by shores and vegetation, the channel seemed to close. "When *Calypso* pokes her snout around that point, she can sink us before we can fairly see her in return! We're helpless."

"Oh now, it's scarce that bad," Hubbard

protested. "With all due respect to both Captain Vane-Templeton and yourself, you each appear to have overlooked something. We may contrive a surprise for him by the time the dawn wind stirs."

The crew, faces showing pallid and strained, were suddenly hanging on his words. Poynter was almost as startled, but disbelieving.

"A surprise?" he demanded. "Now what might all the rest of us have overlooked, which is clear to you?"

"Our little mountain." Hubbard indicated the hill which rose so steeply almost where the entrance-way or exit seemed to close. A part of the eminence showed bare and uninviting, even hostile. Its rocky sides were not unlike the rimrocks from which Vane-Templeton had hailed, rising almost sheer for a hundred feet. By comparison with the higher mountains which loomed in the distance it was little more than a hillock, yet in its way formidable.

"We'll be at need to remove all our guns before we can careen ship to clean it, in any case," Hubbard went on. "Also it would be no more than prudent to have them mounted for defence and to guard against surprise while our *Lively Lady* lies defenseless. So removing them now adds nothing to what

159

must be done, only hurries us a bit in the doing. With perhaps three of our Long Toms emplaced atop that hill, it will require no great skill at gunnery to provide a warm welcome for the *Calypso* when she comes questing."

A sudden wild shout sent a sudden flight of birds bursting from the surrounding greenery, a cheer of relief and triumph as the men understood. Here was an answer so obvious that for that very reason it had been overlooked. But Poynter, his face flaming a deeper red, seemed eager to point out the flaw.

"I've no doubt you're right – providing a trio of such ponderous guns could be there to welcome them by the new day," he conceded. "But will you tell me how that might be done? Those heights are far worse than the cliff you just scaled. Men alone, unhampered, would be hard put to gain the crest. As for hoisting cannon of such weight and ponderous as they are –"

His shrug was eloquent of disbelief.

That he was honest in his doubt Hubbard did not question. He had been made a captain, not from experience or proven ability, but because his father had owned the shipyards. His officers and men had learned by doing, but to him it was inconceivable that cannon of such weight and crankiness could be tugged and hoisted, manhandled up so inhospitable a slope; and certainly not by night or in the time at their disposal.

So certain generals had assumed of a height above the Hudson, during the initial struggle with England; until a rival commander had proved them wrong and rendered their position untenable.

Sullivan stepped forward.

"Don't worry, sir," he said eagerly. "We'll manage – since it's a case of that or, as pirates, having our necks stretched before another sunset. It will be a job, no question of that, but we've plenty of manpower. And Mr. Hubbard's right! With cannon emplaced at that height, we can give the *Calypso* a welcome she'll be far from expecting! We can pound her at point-blank range, with no target in return. By the time she thinks to look for one, the battle will be won!"

TWENTY-ONE

The heat of afternoon was heavy, oppressive, the wind which had so grudgingly assisted them to their anchorage having dropped, even out on the open water. Had it held, Vane-Templeton would have blown in along with it.

Grudgingly, Poynter gave his consent. He pointed out that there was nothing to lose by the attempt, but clearly he doubted that it could succeed; Hubbard was certain that he would almost prefer that it should not, since he could not claim the credit. Denny Poynter had always been a bad loser.

Yet it was reasonable that neither he nor Vane-Templeton, or for that matter any of the others, should have conceived so wildly impossible seeming a plan. Viewing the islands and their channels, the hill was merely one of a number, less inviting than most. Even if the *Calypso*'s captain had considered the possibility, he would like Poynter have rejected it as impossible in the time available to them for putting the plan into execution.

Faced with the alternative should they fail, every man went swiftly to work under Sullivan's direction. As some dismantled a cannon and wrestled it into position, across the deck and to the side for lowering, others lashed a pair of longboats together, joined and strengthened by a platform of planks across both. Even then, they would be heavily burdened, setting low in the water. But it was only a short row across to the hill, so three trips would require no great amount of time.

The task was easy by comparison with emergencies which sometimes came with heavy storms, when a big gun might break loose from its moorings and career wildly, murderously back and forth, with every heave and roll of the ship. Under such conditions, they must be roped and checked at all costs, before pounding everything to hopeless wreckage, then plunging past all restraints and over the side.

With a motionless ship on a calm bay there were no such problems. It was merely a matter of manpower and hard work. While the first gun was being prepared, the boats were sent ahead at Hubbard's suggestion, loaded with ropes and crowbars, with shot and shell and all necessary articles or ordinance. Men not otherwise occupied clawed their way to the hilltop, then proceeded to hoist the supplies into position.

The first big gun was eased to the double deck of the twin craft without mishap, braced solidly, then rowed across the bay. A belated moon, now waning to a grudging half, gave scant light, but sufficient. Stars reflected from the water, swam and bobbed in the ripples. Night sounds, strange to the ears of men long at sea, equally alien to those unaccustomed to the tropics, rose and fell, an eerie accompaniment.

At best the work was slow, innumerable problems cropping up without warning, for which solutions must be found as swiftly. Poynter contented himself with watching, disdaining as captain to lend a hand. Hubbard worked alongside Sullivan. An understanding between them was developing into friendship.

Hoisting the first cannon to the hilltop proved less a chore than some had expected. Pulleys had been brought from the ship, made fast to stout trees on the far side of the hill, and with ropes passed through these, excellent purchase was secured for all who could lay hold on the lines. The big gun swung loose, just above the decks of the longboats, twisted, poised, then ascended.

The second gun was the trouble-maker. It broke loose from its moorings while being lowered from the deck to the longboats, perhaps because of carelessness spawned from the ease with which the first had been handled. It crashed and splintered not only the plank superdeck above one boat, but went through its bottom as well, then was narrowly saved from plunging all the way to the bottom of the sound.

Painfully it was wrestled back in place, smashed planking removed, the ruined boat replaced by the one which still remained to them, and finally it too crossed to the hill.

By then, precious hours had been wasted, and the moon was gone. In the heavier gloom, something slipped and the big gun was a second time in danger of plunging to the sea bottom, saved at the last moment by a sailor who inserted belaying pin and hand alike between slipping rope and spinning pulley, to the detriment alike of pin and hand.

At Hubbard's suggestion, the cooks prepared a hearty meal, and men famished and staggering with weariness were provided a break. The third gun went almost without difficulty. As dawn broke with characteristic abruptness for such latitudes, the blackness replaced by sudden sun and puffs of wind, the third Long Tom was shoved and pulled into place. Hubbard saw to its anchoring, the muzzles of all three set to command the narrow way down which the *Calypso* must venture.

"You seem to be as familiar with guns as with the working of a ship," Sullivan observed. "So, since this was your idea in the first place, you'll be in charge of them."

Hubbard was not adverse. That by making himself useful he was increasing Poynter's resentment rather than gaining his approval was apparent to everyone. But nothing would change that. Poynter was driven by his own resentments, scourged by an unyielding stubbornness along a path from which he was as unwilling as unable to turn.

Bird clamor filled the island, stilled abruptly as the *Calypso* came into view, looming huge and formidable in the narrowness of the channel. As though to afford her every opportunity, the wind held steady. Hubbard nerved himself to a less than welcome task. It seemed almost a sacrilege to batter so brave a ship, but this was war. And her captain had been at pains to emphasize that to surrender or sink were the only alternatives left for the *Lively Lady* and her crew.

Hubbard had seen to the laying of all three guns, a task made easy by the point-blank range. Their first shaking thunder was still in the air when it was matched by a crashing aboard the *Calypso*, a direct hit flinging wreckage in a wild cascade, the destruction obviously far worse than might have been expected. Viewing the results, Hubbard could only conclude that powder and shells had been stacked for ready use, with no thought given to possible risk, and a shell had gotten among the pile. Vane-Templeton had been sure that his prey was helpless.

The ball from the gun next in line had smashed the mainmast in almost a replica of the injury suffered earlier by the *Lively Lady*, bringing it crashing, with a smothering crush of sails. Both hits had been lucky, though their devastation would have been matched with a continuous hail. Crippled, not able to loose off a shot in return, the *Calypso* was floundering, striving desperately to turn, to retreat.

Sullivan was dancing with excitement, his usual calm as shattered as the enemy. At such moments battle became a struggle more of giant forces than of men; they became like puppets, impelled almost to madness.

"Sink him!" Sullivan screamed. "Blow them to hell! Another round will do it."

He might be right, even if so sturdy a ship, however badly hurt, was far from going down. Hubbard drew back, shaking his head. Eyes and teeth gleamed white through a mask of powder smoke.

"That's what we don't want," he pointed out. "With the channel blocked, we'd be trapped."

Sullivan swung, blinking, as though seeing him for the first time. His head-shake was between admiration and disbelief.

"You're right," he admitted. "But don't you ever get excited? I'd forgotten all about that."

Half of the *Lively Lady* crew had climbed and scrambled to vantage points on the hill or along its sides. On the point of cheering, they sat sobered instead as those aboard the stricken vessel labored frantically. Halting though the process, they succeeded in turning, putting about, finally limping from sight.

"It'll be a while before she can fight again," Sullivan observed. Reflecting on their own immobilization, as opposed to the destruction of an enemy, he was cheerful. His grin grew more expansive at a sudden thought. He'd counted himself as directing, under Poynter. Actually, Hubbard had been the one in command.

Poynter was not among those clustered on the hill. Aloof as usual, he had remained aboard the *Lively Lady*. On their return he commended Sullivan for a job well done. Hubbard he ignored.

Sullivan bristled like a hedgehog.

"What I did was routine. The plan and its execution, clear to the destruction of the enemy, were the work of Mr. Hubbard."

Poynter's awareness that Sullivan had omitted the customary "sir" blazed in suddenly hot cheeks. He overlooked the slight in a larger rebuke.

"If you feel that no credit accrues to you, Sullivan, then no doubt you're right," he said icily, and swung away. The atmosphere of victory was smothered like fog closing across the bay.

Sullivan turned to the watching, now uncertain crew. His were the instincts of an officer.

"It has been a long night, and a hard. You've earned your rest." Catching Hubbard's eye, he checked in mid-sentence. "You have something in mind, Mr. Hubbard?"

"We are faced now with a matter of time," Hubbard pointed out. "At best, we have little enough of it. Tired we all are, but I can do a day's work, for as long as the light lasts. As between extra toil now, or a hangnoose later, I doubt there's question of choice in any man's mind."

Mr. Sandys, the second officer, pulled at a long chin.

"When you put it that way, Mr. Hubbard, of course you're right. Yet for the curiosity of all of us, why is time so pressing? In the unlikely event of another visitor, we could hold off a fleet, with those guns on the hill. And the *Calypso* will be some time licking her wounds."

"That she will," Hubbard conceded. "But she retains a couple of masts, and will rig more in a matter of hours. She's still a sailing ship, and will soon enough be a fighting ship

169

again, while one thought drives every man aboard her, and that notion – revenge! Should she manage to return, as belike she may, with a companion, and from her standpoint, hopefully before we can regain the open sea –" His shrug was expressive.

Sullivan stroked his chin in turn. Here again was forethought beyond his own reckoning, or the calculations of Denny Poynter. In any such match the odds would favor the British. Days, even a few hours, might reverse the issue.

"I couldn't sleep by daylight," Sandys' grin was contagious. "Let's about it, then."

Poynter had paced to the far limit of the quarter-deck, turning from there to listen. He scowled and went below.

Tropic sun from a cloudless sky was new to most of them, the air heavy and humid. Shirts were discarded, followed in some instances by every article of clothing. That made it easy to slip into the water overside, to temper the burn of the sun. To the astonishment of most, Hubbard, though doing his full share, retained his shirt. One ventured a question.

"Beggin' your pardon, sir, but how do you stand it? I used to think I knew what hot was, in a summer along the Sound – but this! It's as though the door to hell had been left open."

"It's just that I find it cooler with something to keep the sun from bare skin," Hubbard explained. "Tomorrow, most of you will understand. A burn deep in the flesh is worse."

Some few took heed to his warning, donning their shirts again. Most shrugged unbelievingly. The frequent dips overside had a tempering effect, but Hubbard had learned, as a boy on a raft, the dangers of double burn of sun on water.

He swam across to the rimrocks and clambered to the crest, to stare where the small boat had danced the day before. The *Calypso* was a dwindling speck against the horizon. But she sailed well, all things considered, moreover ports for repairs were scattered among the islands, some of which would provide a welcome.

Poynter was going ashore as he returned to the *Lively Lady*, stepping on to the beach. He had voiced no interference with Sullivan or his orders, but neither was he taking part. His philosophy, unchanged, had been voiced as a boy.

"Menial chores are for menials. Never for a captain."

Hubbard saw his stiffen suddenly, his eyes on the wall of greenery whence the little creek crept out. Excitement mantled Poynter's face

171

and throat, like the sudden panting of a hound at sight of prey. A woman, almost certainly the one who had made those tracks in the sand, had stepped into view.

TWENTY-TWO

Hubbard had come to know Poynter well, so that reading his mind under such circumstances was no more of a problem than skimming a printed sheet. Poynter had gone ashore with the hope of flushing the woman from her covert, questing like a dog with the scent of fox or partridge in its nostrils.

Perhaps for a measure of protection against the sun, more probably with thought of the impression he might make, Poynter wore a wide-brimmed hat, elegantly styled. He raised a hand to doff it, back beginning a supple bend, both motions checked at the half-point. His eyes, always inclined to protuberance, goggled.

The mystery woman was before him, but not, as he had so hopefully envisioned. Here was scarcely an island goddess, not even a woodland nymph.

Others aboard and around the *Lively Lady* were turning to stare as well, impelled like their captain by more than curiosity, surprised alike if not so shocked. If indeed fair lady was to be discovered, Denny Poynter would be first to assert superior rights.

That she was a white woman was apparent, more from bare feet and ankles peeping beneath a soiled and ragged dress than from arms or face. Somehow it was the dream, perhaps a natural expectation of every man, that a woman, whether native to an island paradise or a castaway upon its shores, should be young and at the least comely. But women, like men, grow older, and not all were endowed even in youth with good looks. This creature, to judge by what the eye revealed, was plentifully supplied with years, but had never been much favored in the way of beauty.

Her hair, still dark, was disordered. Beneath it the face had an anxious look, one with hope but short on expectancy. Years, combined with the ravages of sun and grime, combined for an effect less than pleasing, even to an undiscriminating eye. And Poynter had clearly brought himself to a point of high expectancy.

He took a backward step, dismay, almost abhorrence, replacing the avid gleam in his eyes. The woman's speech came falteringly, as though her tongue had grown unused to it.

"Sir – oh, sir – I've watched – I have been so frightened."

Poynter overcame his disappointment. He had been trained as a gentleman, even if possessing few such instincts. Pity, a vague sympathy, replaced repugnance. Their voices came clearly to those on board as he assured her that she had no cause for apprehension, then drew from her fragments of her story.

Though not quite incoherent, she was far from clear. Apparently she had been cast away on the island quite a while before, a point of time about which she was vague. She had managed to subsist.

Her name, she recalled uncertainly, was Connie. Constance. Somehow it clashed with its possessor.

Poynter could glean no more, nor did he try very hard. Apparently she was well enough with quarters somewhere on the island. His proffer of food from the ship's supplies she accepted with an eagerness bordering on the pathetic, but declined a suggestion to come aboard. Presently, supplied with freshly cooked food sufficient for several meals, she bobbed her head in a dimly remembered curtsy, then vanished. Poynter, mopping a flushed face, was clearly relieved to have her go.

"The poor devil!" he muttered, his tone still incredulous. "But what a witch!"

The men were grinning and shaking their heads. Denny Poynter, to those who had known him ashore, had considered himself something of a dandy, a ladies' man. He had aspired to the daughter of a Marquis, centering his affections on Renee. The manner of her leave-taking from the *Lively Lady*, with no word of farewell, had shocked and infuriated. He could not but account her dead, at least to himself, and the odds were strong for such reality.

Hurt pride had left his heart untouched. That had been clear to Hubbard from the first. Such affection as he possessed Denny had bestowed upon Renee, and if for him there was a lodestar she was far out in front, even as her likeness skimmed the seas at the bows of the *Lively Lady*. But the only person that Denny Poynter had ever loved or was capable of loving was himself.

He kept to his cabin for the remainder of the day, shocked and disillusioned.

What they had witnessed was salutary for the crew. Hubbard had sensed the leashed eagerness among them, remembering the small, perfectly formed footprints. Now there would be no stealing away to quest the island stealthily, each for himself. They would give full effort to the work to be done.

Much had been accomplished that day, the remainder of the guns moved painfully to the shore. Experience had helped, and though a petty officer had cursed bitterly when a cannon had broken away and plunged into the sea, it had been a comparatively small loss. All had to be moved prior to the careening.

Hubbard's prophecy of sunburn and its painful effects was fulfilled before the day was out. Backs, torsos, arms and neck took on the hue of boiled lobsters. Men cringed and winced. They smeared one another with grease provided from the stores, some shrinking even from a light touch; others, darker of skin and pigment, jeered at their fellows and suffered no more than a passing inconvenience. By the next day, at least a handful would be incapacitated, perhaps for a week.

He went ashore, intent on stretching on the swiftly cooling sands of the beach. Sullivan was ahead of him. Hubbard questioned,

"I suppose you're posting a watch at the hilltop? Even men asleep there will form a guard – probably not really necessary. But with the existence of such a battery known, we'd be in bad shape should anyone think to return even in a small boat and take possession."

Sullivan came to an elbow, staring from eyes bemused by fatigue. Then he came groaningly to his feet.

"You're right. You think of everything. I hadn't – and Poynter's said nothing." His tone was eloquent of disgust. "I'll get a few others and go there for tonight."

With the morning, Hubbard's expectation that the worst cases of sunburn, which had approached stroke, would be unable to work, were confirmed. Poynter, suddenly alert to his duties, cursed them for malingering, but not even the threat of the cat could stir them. Sullivan pointed out that they were clearly incapable of work, and Poynter grudgingly acquiesced. He kept mostly to the shade.

But his eyes, when they turned toward Hubbard, burned with a malignancy to rival the sun.

Lieutenant Sandys, next in rank below Sullivan, proved more knowledgeable than all the rest as to the proper careening of a ship. Diffidently he explained that he had taken part in such an operation, not many years before, and his memory was retentive.

With only stumps of masts remaining, and the guns removed, it was easy work by comparison to unload remaining stores and goods. While that went on, the island must be explored, big trees found and cut, both for masts and other repairs. Leaving details at the ship to Mr. Sandys, Sullivan and Hubbard set out to look over the island.

"Poynter suggested at first that he'd do all this, but as soon as he discovered that there was no native beauty to hunt down, he seems to have forgotten about it," Sullivan confided. "In any case, I'll prefer your judgment to his."

Hubbard looked forward to such exploration, to the shade of great trees as opposed to the heat of the sun. But the lifeless heat under their canopy was hardly an improvement. If not jungle, it was not far removed, and while in some respects these Indies came close to paradise, in others they fell far short.

This island, more than a mile long by half as much in width, at least contained what they were most in need of. On a higher slope was a stand of great trees. Selecting a few of the best, sawyers and axe-men were set to felling and trimming.

Not far beyond, come upon abruptly as they broke from growth lush to the edge, another rocky cliff fell away, sheer for a hundred feet. Under an almost too-benign sun the sea showed grim and inhospitable.

Under the rasp of storm it would be less than friendly to any ships.

Stripped and showing less lovely by comparison, the *Lively Lady* slipped her anchor cables, to be swarmed by waiting boats, hauled to the beach and on to it. Trees at the green fringe served as anchors for ropes and cables, used for warping the great ship in and up.

The men who had been made ill by near sunstroke were now sufficiently recovered to work again, and crews took turns, sweating, toiling at the capstan, circling it slowly, hawsers squeaking and straining as the cables wound ever tighter. The easy gradient helped, assisted by deep water almost to the shore line, then soft sand. But as the water shallowed, it was slow, bitter toil before they could make use of rollers. After that the action eased.

Poynter still remained largely aloof, now and then making a tour of inspection, issuing an occasional order. Aware that he was less and less the commander, disliked and mistrusted, he cannily avoided any word or action which might precipitate a crisis.

Once the ship was high and dry, one side was exposed. Weeds and barnacles encrusted her bottom, the everlasting vexation of every shipmaster. As they increased, a vessel's speed and maneuverability lessened.

With the *Lady* basking in the sun, it was a good start. A couple of days of heat would dry the foulness to the point where the growth could be scraped and burned away, a tiresome chore but vital. While she was drying the men could enjoy a well-earned rest.

The saw and axe crews had done equally well, felling and fashioning trees, tugging and sliding them to the beach.

Time was passing, but they were well to the schedule which the more knowledgeable had set. Mindful that the *Calypso* might attain greater speed in a regular shipyard, then very likely return with a companion ship, none were inclined to loiter unnecessarily.

Lounging in shade and unaccustomed idleness, Sullivan surveyed the beach spread before them, with its stream of clear water, with mild approval.

"Not bad," he confided. "Could be a lot worse, as a place to be stranded – as that poor old woman is. She certainly keeps to herself, and I guess you could say that improves the scenery. I can see why the pirates used to like it here."

"Did they?" Hubbard was not much interested.

"That's what Stamford claims. Says he had that from his grandfather, who I take it was one of them. He claims it was a more or less regular rendezvous – and may still be, for that matter. *We're* not the only pirates," he added significantly.

Hubbard recalled seeing Stamford in earnest conversation with Poynter. The oddity there lay in Poynter deigning to notice a mere crewman. But perhaps he was feeling the growing isolation, even from his officers.

Sullivan was technically and legally correct. They were pirates, though differing from most of that ilk in that, New England born and bred, they had the ingrained habit of hard work and thrift.

To Hubbard, work kept him occupied, leaving less time to think, to ponder an unpromising situation; most of all, to wonder about Renee, whether or not she had survived, and if so sudden a voyage had helped, or only worsened an already impossible situation.

Even if she still lived, the chance of his finding her again was slight. It was not a subject to dwell on, but he could not put it from his mind. Without Renee, what happened to himself did not greatly matter.

Cleaning the hull from its encrustations proved as tedious a business under a tropic sun as any of them had found it on other conditions in more temperate climes. The reflection that winter must be sending gale winds and driving snow across Long Island Sound was unable to cool them. Most of the crew were tanning to a brownness to rival loaves fresh from the oven. The initial cases of sunburn had healed, but sweat poured from pores like the rush of the little creek to join the bay.

Those not busy with scraping were kept busy, shaping masts and timbers for the repairs to follow. Hubbard's warning as to the possible return of the *Calypso* was taken seriously.

Restless, Hubbard prowled the island, his mind increasingly on the impossible, fruits forbidden or out of reach. Snow. A fire of crackling logs. Maple syrup. Home.

And Renee. Always Renee. However impossible, until recently he'd had the dream. Now even that was shattered, gone. Sighing, he stretched in a shady spot, but sleep would not come. Mid-afternoon marked a period of unbearable heat. Even those who could work on the shady side of the careened ship had to desist for a while.

Impatiently he went on, to check, surprised, at a glimpse of something white. Briefly seen and as swiftly gone, it was not a bird and could hardly be an animal. Leafy undergrowth made a screen. Here the trees grew tall, allowing little sun to penetrate. Among them the underbrush was rare, as was anything lower than the high branches.

His curiosity stirred, Hubbard worked closer, and the screen of brush was explained. There was a small, natural clearing. Almost free of trees, it allowed other growth. He checked a second time, breath in check, in sudden if only partial understanding.

A small spring, enshrouded by greenery, fed a deep pool. And in that, seeking relief from the sticky heat, in so remote an amphitheatre, someone was bathing. Even spring water would be no more than pleasantly cool on such a day.

Proof of his deduction was the sight of an arm, golden brown below the elbow but a marble white above, smoothly rounded. As his breath quickened he made out a torso, below a face curiously streaked and blotched; unsightly as it was, it was suggestive not of age and decrepitude but of youth, perhaps even beauty. He drew a breath of understanding.

The old woman of the island, whom they had seen briefly but rarely, was bathing at this remote and unsuspected spot, luxuriating in its coolness. That was a certainty. Just as surely, she who occupied the pool was young, not at all the distressful crone which she had seemed.

TWENTY-THREE

Hubbard's feet moved almost of their own volition, then he checked in sudden confusion. He had blundered on this hideaway, chancing there at a moment when the girl was enjoying the privacy of a bath, understandably apprehensive of discovery should she make use of the bay or creek.

His New England training forbade spying, still his feet remained rooted to the spot. All that was visible from his vantage point was her head and face, alabaster arms and shoulders, a throat soft and round and wrinkle-free, even as was the curiously mottled face. He judged that she was either sitting in the pool, or perhaps standing in water up to her waist.

At the moment her profile was to him, her attitude intent, almost startled. She seemed to be looking at something in the pool, and he recognized what it must be. She had splashed about, reveling in the coolness, momentarily forgetful of mundane details. But now, as she had paused long enough for the water to calm

184

to its usual mirror-like aspect, she must have caught a glimpse of herself, of the disfiguring blotchiness which marred her face.

All at once she was scrubbing vigorously at it with both hands. Then, as she straightened, partially turning, Hubbard saw her face, washed clean, and again his breath was sharply indrawn. As he had already guessed, she was young, girlishly beautiful, the antithesis of what she had appeared. Red lips parted above perfect teeth, a cascade of dark hair was flung back from rounded shoulder and arm.

She smiled, then frowned at her reflection, pleased but not quite approving. Certainly there was enough to enchant the eye of almost any beholder, a face and figure to excite admiration. Hubbard was beginning to understand.

One part of her story had been true; certainly she was a castaway. Beyond that were certain fabrications. Watching the approach of the *Lively Lady*, its intrusion into her lonely Eden, beholding its state of damage and guessing its purpose, to anchor for weeks while repairs were made, she had of course been apprehensive. Scores of men would soon swarm over the island. Since her footprints were already in the sands, to hide from their almost certain hunt would be difficult if not impossible.

Her wit, along with skills undoubtedly acquired in at least a sizeable settlement, had come to her aid. Clearly she possessed a knowledge of stains compounded from barks and berries, with the addition of mud and grime, of bits of half-rotten leafage to lend an impression of toothlessness. Working with the mirror of a pool or perhaps a glass, she had made up face, hands and arms to the illusion not only of age, but of homeliness which bordered on the repulsive.

Her ruse had worked, Denny Poynter, as eager on the hunt as any of his crew might prove, had started back in dismay at sight of such a crone. There had been no question in anyone's mind as to the reality of what they saw.

Probably she had been careful not to wash her face since then, making sure that the disguise remained intact. But today, at this remote spot, sweaty from the extreme heat, she had reveled in the coolness of the water, forgetting the disguise which she could not see. Only after it had washed and run had she sensed its ruin.

At the moment she was rejoicing in restored beauty. The make-up could be repaired.

Reluctant at the necessity, she was starting to climb from the pool. Hubbard, with matching reluctance, turned his back to move away. He felt a strong surge of admiration for her wit and skill, and he had no intention of intruding on her privacy.

A startled cry, sharp against the silence, turned him as quickly back. In it was terror and dismay.

A glance was enough for Hubbard to understand.

If chance sometimes stretched the arm of coincidence, such things happened. He had not been the only one to happen this way, or to catch sight of the girl. Denny Poynter fronted her, face to face, the avid leer in eyes and manner as repulsive to Hubbard as they clearly were to the girl.

After her initial outcry she fronted him, apprehensive but far from intimidated, though looking about wildly for a way of escape. Foreseeing such a reaction, Poynter had chosen his moment well. Heavy brush grew at either side, too thick to break through, even had she been clothed against its brambles. There remained only the pool, and she stepped quickly back and in, immersing herself to her shoulders.

"Go away!" she panted, and now there was no faltering in her speech. "Are you no gentleman?"

Poynter's retort was triumphant and characteristic.

"I'm called a pirate, which I suppose I am. So why shouldn't I behave like one?"

The girl was suddenly calm, dangerous as a cornered creature of the jungle.

"If I have to, I'll kill you," she warned, and it was a promise rather than a threat.

Poynter, his face inflamed from more than the heat, laughed. In half-opened mouth, darting eyes and twitching fingers his eagerness showed, fast mounting past restraint. Having accounted her old and a hag, he now made the mistake of taking the extreme opposite, that as a woman she would faint or swoon.

"Hold on, Connie, I'm coming!" The shout was as startling to Hubbard as to Poynter, followed by an instant crashing through the brush. A man, tall as Hubbard, softly bearded, unsuspected by the ship's company during its tenancy of the island, caused Poynter to turn, barely in time to front the newcomer.

"That won't be necessary," he added, his words to the girl but attention all for Poynter. "*I'll* kill him."

That might be neither idle threat nor boastfulness. Like Poynter, he carried a sword, not an article of adornment but one intended for the duello, for defense or attack.

TWENTY-FOUR

Slackening jaw and backing step attested Denny Poynter's dismay. He had accounted his conquest as all but complete, the girl's defiance no more than was to be expected of a maiden in such a plight, but even if real readily to be overcome. The others on the island were his crew, and far away. Even if any might have strayed this far, to challenge or thwart him would be mutiny. An offence punishable by death.

The sudden appearance of the man, the certainty that he intended exactly what he promised, was unsettling. But Poynter's blood was hot with more than the sun, and he counted himself adept with the weapon he carried.

The other man's sword was a dazzling streak of silver in the sun. Almost as swiftly, Poynter's sword was in his hand, and he wasted neither time nor courtesy with the foolishness of preliminaries. As he swung he lunged, a murderous ruse which possessed the merit of surprise, of taking an opponent off-balance, frequently ending a contest before it was well begun.

With most opponents it would have succeeded, but it became plain that this man, like the woman, was more than met the eye at initial glance. If not from the expectancy of such murderous trickery, he read Poynter's intention in his eyes, always a signal of intent a fraction of an instant ahead of the stroke. He took a single step to the side, and Poynter's driving thrust found only air. The extremity of his effort all but threw him off-balance.

Contemptuously almost, the other man disdained to avail himself of the chance to run Poynter through his back before he could sidestep or recover. Wary, face drained of blood, Poynter recovered, feinted with blinding speed, drove again. The blades clashed and rang.

Both men were avid for the kill, but the one was a gentleman, who played by the rules of the game. Castaways though he and the girl were, their quality was manifest. Against such a man as Poynter, it was a mistake.

Poynter had disdained the suggestion that he might be a gentleman, and he proved it anew with a cunning stroke taught him by some swordsman of more than usual ability. The blades seemed to embrace, to cling together for a breathless moment. Then, so suddenly that all three, rendered now as spectators – Hubbard, the girl and her

190

champion, could only stare as the one blade clattered to the ground.

Poynter had disarmed his opponent with a swiftness which clearly left him as surprised as any. In it there had undoubtedly been more of luck than skill. But such things could happen. His laugh was a wild crow of triumph.

"So you'd cross steel with me, would you?" he taunted. "With Poynter of the *Savage!* You'd kill me, I mind you bragged. Well, a killing there'll be, if not quite as you intended."

Again he lunged, and the other man stood a moment, his face twisting between pain and incredulity, transfixed. Poynter's blade was buried almost to the hilt, the point protruding from his back.

The girl gasped in terror and dismay. Poynter laughed again, the sound as horrible as the bubble staining the sweaty shirt of his victim, front and back.

"So much for your lover," he said contemptuously. "Or for any fool who gets in my way. But don't let it distress your pretty head. You've found a better man in his place."

"Murderer!" The girl managed the word through unsteady lips, her accent once again faltering. "He was not my lover. He's my brother."

191

Brother or not, sorely stricken, the injured man swayed, then collapsed. The girl screamed, then surged wildly from the haven of the pool, forgetful in that instant of her own condition, to run and fall on her knees beside him.

Poynter stared, taken aback at such a revelation, his triumph tempered by so unlooked-for a turn.

"I – I didn't –" he began, to stare with mounting consternation as Hubbard confronted him.

"Murder it was," Hubbard informed him, and stooped suddenly to snatch up the fallen sword. "But it will be no murder to kill you as I'm about to do, Denny – only justice and retribution."

Startled in her turn, the girl stared wild-eyed, but neither Poynter nor Hubbard had time or attention for her at the moment. Poynter was appalled. Events were moving at a speed beyond his liking, and the knowledge that he had struck down the girl's brother, and in so murderous a manner – that he was brother rather than husband or lover, left him shaken. The additional advent of Hubbard was even worse.

Poynter stared, then hate came to his rescue. What was done was done, and reflection assured him that from his point of view it was none so ill. True enough, the stroke had been sheer murder, against a man unarmed and unsuspecting, but it had merely hurried what in any case would have been certain necessity. Whether with weapon in hand or not, it had to be done.

And in the long run the girl's hate would be no greater.

He had not counted on Hubbard, but this furnished the excuse for which Poynter had been hoping. Rancor had built with each day in which he watched the increasing admiration and respect accorded his long-time rival; a situation too dangerous to be allowed to continue.

Always the object of his dislike, Hubbard now had become a menace. Now he had not only an excuse but a reason for taking action. A man must defend himself.

Poynter was confident. The girl's brother appeared to have been a skilled swordsman, but he had overcome him with surprising ease. Hubbard, on the other hand, and so far as he had ever heard, was no better than a novice, so should be even less of a problem.

Hubbard's heat matched the sun's, but as always, he had an almost detached coolness when a fight impended. He retreated to the clear spot where there was room for maneuver, Poynter following leisurely, with an air of disdain. His increasing certainty of a double triumph was a powerful restorative.

"What could be more fitting or natural?" he asked. "You and I, Bran! I've always known that it would come to this, sooner or later. We've always hated each other, and you've always contrived, with the luck of the devil, to stand in my way. But I've always intended to kill you, and now is the time."

Again he essayed the murderous trick which had worked so well, a sudden lunging rush, even as he appeared to look skyward. Again it failed, more disastrously. Somehow Hubbard met the darting stroke with a beating, parrying smash, and as the other man's blade had been twisted from his grasp, so was Poynter's jarred loose. Steel rang against a rock, the sound like a knell.

Dumbfounded, Poynter stared. His arm hung limp, numbed to the elbow. Terror, as stark as the sick apprehension which had swum in the girl's eyes, drove the sullen heat from his face, replaced by a washed-out flabbiness as Hubbard advanced.

"I should run you through as you did him," he gritted. "Kill you I will. But pick up your weapon. Defend yourself – if you can."

With a contemptuous kick he sent Poynter's sword toward him, almost to his feet. The glittering steel was a temptation. Poynter stared at it, half-stooping, his fingers twitching, then drew back. His gaze now was on the point of the blade in Hubbard's hand, holding him as if mesmerized. Along with it he could see the set face above, lips bared from hard-clamped teeth.

Too well he knew that look, the implacable will behind it. Poynter's memory went back to fights, to boyish battles, contests, which by every rule of age and strength he should have won, yet which had ended in defeat, sometimes humiliating, always with a nature of inevitability.

He jerked his eyes away, looking down, then back. Terror which he had assured himself was long conquered stifled like heartburn. If he picked up the sword he would die on the point of another. Yet the look on Hubbard's face allowed no hope for a middle ground. For Hubbard this was no longer personal. Fate had given him the role of executioner.

A sob, half-bleat, broke from Poynter's lips. He turned, running wildly. Moments later, to Hubbard's astonishment, he was gone, vanishing in a wild leap over the suddenly revealed crest of rocky cliff. A hundred feet below the sea washed sullenly.

TWENTY-FIVE

Hubbard checked his rush to stare, more startled by the nearness of the ocean than by the desperate choice of Poynter. Somehow it was in keeping. Poynter was not a coward, but faced with the certainty of the fate he had meted to another man, it was not surprising that he would choose the untender mercies of the sea.

Any ship would lie becalmed, the air breathless with the heat. The waters showed placid, empty.

Recollecting, Hubbard swung back. The girl crouched beside her brother's outsprawled lankness, lifting eyes tear-stained and desperate.

"Can you do anything?" she pleaded. "Or is – is he –"

Hubbard dropped to his own knees, his attention studiously for Poynter's victim. That he was already dead he had no doubt, for the blow had been intended to kill, enhanced as Poynter had jerked his blade back and loose, starting the blood gushing alike from back and chest. Still the pleading in the girl's eyes was not to be denied.

To Hubbard's surprise, there was a heartbeat. Death, like life, traveled no set trail.

That it could be long stayed was doubtful, but he had seen others in bloody estate, had labored over them and learned something from experience. Since the initial thrust had failed to kill, apparently no vital parts had been reached. If the bleeding could be stanched, there was at least a possibility for recovery. Reason enough to do what he could, even without the beseeching look in the eyes of the girl.

Eyes bright even through the blue of tears, a piquant face formed for mischief rather than grief.

The initial step was simple and easy of accomplishment. A mossy boulder made up one side of the pool, immediately at hand. He tore off chunks of the moss, thrusting them into the wounds at either side, holding them in place with both hands. They made effectual pads, the bleeding quickly slowed to a trickle.

"He'll have to have a bandage, one clear around his body, a cloth tied tight to hold those plugs in place," Hubbard explained, not looking up. "I've got to hold them from loosening until it can be managed. If you can get my shirt off me –"

"I'll do better than that." The girl was

swift to comprehend. Judging by the manner in which she had disguised herself, such decisiveness was not surprising. "Wait, I won't be long."

Though studiously refraining from looking up, Hubbard was aware that she had darted away. He judged that she must be hurrying to where her own clothes had been piled.

She was back faster than he had expected, and from the first sidelong glance he saw that she had donned the somewhat shapeless garment which had clothed her as a supposedly infirm and toothless hag.

In her hand she clutched other garments, one a long white and dainty creation which he suspected had been next to her skin. It was of excellent material, neither soiled nor torn.

She studied the situation an instant, lower lip full and scarlet where it was caught between teeth white and even. With surprising strength she tore a long, wide strip, then another.

Dropping to her knees, her face was close to Hubbard's, her breath soft against his cheek. With no show of emotion she wound one strip around her brother's ribs and chest, as Hubbard lifted him a few inches, loosening one hand at a time for the cloth to be fitted. Presently both strips were in place and tied, forming a close bandage. Hubbard

198

was relieved that scarcely a trace of blood showed as he lowered the wounded man back to the ground. Thanks to the girl's skill, the bandage was working well.

Only then did she meet his eyes, a touch of color returning to her cheeks, question large in her own.

"Do you think – does he have a chance?"

The heartbeat remained surprisingly strong. Hubbard nodded.

"At least a chance," he conceded. "I'll get back to the ship, bring men and blankets and a stretcher. With good care, it's at least a possibility."

"I can never thank you enough for – for everything." Beyond that she wasted no words. "I'll stay with him. Please hurry. It will be very dark soon after sunset."

That left little time to spare, since to make their way in heavy gloom would be all but impossible. Hubbard set off at once, staring again from the point where Poynter had jumped, at the lazy yet sullen wash of the sea. In either direction the cliffs rose sheer and inhospitable.

The day's developments had been swiftly savage, unpredictable. Somehow it was in keeping.

He reached the beach, where the work went forward, men taking advantage of the slight coolness after siesta during the hottest part of the afternoon. Sullivan walked cat-like on the crest of the upturned vessel. He descended promptly at Hubbard's hail.

"Back about a mile we have a badly injured man, and he should be gotten here before dark. I'll explain as we return. We'll need a door, padded with blankets, and half a dozen men to carry it."

Characteristically, Sullivan did not ask questions. Within minutes, they were on the way back, half a dozen other men in the rear. Sullivan's glance was quizzical.

"I could be mistaken, of course, but even as you showed up, I'd been talking to the men, giving them a bit of credit for the job they're doing, at the same time making sure that everyone was present and accounted for. They all were – except for Poynter and yourself."

"The injured man is a stranger to the rest of us. He's the brother of that girl we saw the other day."

"That a girl should have a brother is within reason. But a girl that we saw the other day –" Sullivan's brows lifted incredulously. "You can hardly be referring to the woman we saw. Even by stretching a point, in the interests of gallantry –"

"You'll understand when you see her again. Poynter surprised her – bathing. She screamed. I'm of the opinion that she could have taken care of herself, but at her outcry, her brother appeared. Armed, and ready for anything. There was a fight. The luck was with Poynter. He disarmed his opponent."

"And wounded him in the process?"

"No. That came as the brother stood, disarmed and unsuspecting. Poynter ran him through."

Save for another lift of the eyebrows, Sullivan showed no surprise.

"But he's still alive?"

"And hopefully may remain so."

Sullivan moved some distance in silence, digesting what he had heard.

"You didn't leave Poynter and the girl to watch him – together." It was statement rather than question.

"Poynter escaped me, by jumping into the sea."

Sullivan's brows arched a third time, but not in surprise. He did not pursue the subject.

"This girl – and her brother. The more you tell me, the less I understand."

"They're castaways, clearly. Where they came from, why, or how long – there was no time for questions. As to the lady herself, I've a notion that somewhere she learned the art of make-up, perhaps acting in amateur entertainments. You had a look at her, so will concede that she did an excellent job, wanting a disguise for obvious reasons. As she was bathing, along with the extreme heat, the grim and colors washed and ran, so she cleaned them away completely. After which, by ill chance, Poynter came upon her."

Sullivan's tone was suddenly vicious.

"It's too bad you didn't kill him – you, or her brother."

"We tried." As they reached the point where the greenery gave way to island's end, he pointed to the sea far below. "He jumped from there."

Sullivan blinked with understanding. In his head-shake was almost a touch of sympathy.

"With you after him, I'm not too surprised. I'd have done the same."

For all the warning which Hubbard had given, his eyes widened at sight of the girl. Beholding her against the fast-lowering sun. Hubbard decided that she might be more than twenty, but not by much. Even the decrepit dress could not hide her beauty.

The stretcher-bearers, who had not been in hearing, stared in sheer astonishment, but no time was lost in lifting and sliding the unconscious man on to the stretcher. They began the journey back. There had been no change in condition that Hubbard could detect.

Hubbard led, a hand on the corner of the door, the girl alongside. Everyone remained silent, partly from bewilderment. Sullivan made a suggestion.

"I'll run ahead and have a shelter rigged, near the creek and at the edge of the beach. He'll need shade by day, along with protection from the rain."

He had an awning rigged by the time they arrived, while several men were gathering grass and ferns to make mattresses. It had already grown too dark for the bewildered crewmen to form any opinion of the girl, but the report was running like wildfire, garbled snatches from the stretcher-bearers. Having beheld her, they attributed almost the qualities of an island goddess to such unexpected beauty.

Showing weary from strain and apprehension, she shared supper with Hubbard and Sullivan. Forewarned, the cooks had been at pains to prepare as tasty a meal as they could manage, making use of the ship's stores. She exclaimed appreciatively.

"It has been months since I've had such a meal. Fruit and sea food, even roasted fish, are nourishing enough, but after a while they have a terrible sameness."

"You've been here for some while then, Ma'am?" Sullivan asked politely.

"A couple of months, as nearly as I can judge. Eight of us were out for a sail, from another island. It was a perfect day. Then a storm struck, with almost no warning. We were driven helplessly for hours, and finally the boat went down."

Firelight reflected on the planes of her face, showing wistful and thoughtful.

"I didn't suppose that any of us could survive, but Ralph is a strong swimmer. With his help, I reached shore here."

Quietly she added their names. Ralph and Constance O'Hara. Sullivan exclaimed,

"It's doubly pleased I am to meet you, Miss O'Hara. With a name as Irish as my own."

Her half-seen smile was ambiguous.

"After three generations among the islands, I'm afraid our name is the only part which remains Irish."

Morning brought hope. Ralph awoke, conscious. Hubbard could detect no fever. Of his own experience, he did not subscribe too strongly to the custom of many surgeons to bleed a patient on any and nearly all occasions, but at least O'Hara seemed to have suffered no ill-effects from the blood-letting. There appeared a reasonable chance that by the time the *Lively Lady* should be ready for the sea, he would be well enough to go aboard as a passenger.

With breakfast out of the way, Sullivan called the men to attention. That the meeting was on sparkling white sand rather than the deck of the *Lively Lady* made little difference. They had enlisted as navy men, a privateer's crew, and even with the changes of a year, discipline remained ingrained.

"You're wondering just what happened, and you deserve straight answers," Sullivan said without preamble, and gave them the substance of what Hubbard had told him the day before. No one showed surprise or shock. Relief was on most faces. Poynter had been their captain, and for a time, even after he had tricked and led them along forbidden ways, they had followed with a degree of enthusiasm. The success and profits of early adventures had offset doubts.

But when he had turned to preying on American ships, when they found themselves branded traitors and pirates, most had had second thoughts. The rub had been that it was too late to turn back. With nowhere else to go, their only salvation had lain in following Poynter where he chose to lead.

"That's the situation," Sullivan added. "And it affects all of us. Primarily in that we are without a captain."

Hubbard intervened.

"You become captain by virtue of your

position, Mr. Sullivan. I'm sure no one will question your right."

"I appreciate your confidence, but I question my competence for command under the circumstances with which we are confronted," Sullivan returned. "But for you, we'd have come to grief long since. As first mate of the *Red Savage,* you become automatically captain of this ship which has to remain the *Red Savage* or become fair prey for every other ship afloat. But as a matter of form, I'm asking every man to ratify your accession to command, Captain Hubbard."

TWENTY-SIX

A ragged but enthusiastic cheer greeted his pronouncement. As Poynter had sensed since their arrival at the harbor, the *Lively Lady*'s crew had been prepared to demand such a change. They had come to admire Hubbard; even more to the point, he if anyone might save them from the tightening noose which Poynter had set about their throats.

Hubbard wasted no time with pious disclaimers.

"If that's the way you want it, I'll do my

best, since my own neck is in equal jeopardy. I've no need to remind you of the dangers we face. Fortunately, our ship is known and accepted now as the *Red Savage,* and the evil reputation which Poynter sought to foist upon the *Savage* has rebounded against the *Lively Lady.* It has been a shameful matter, more especially against once honest ships or one with such a name.

"Since the sinking of the *Lively Lady,* followed by the brush with the Dutchman, our skirmishes have been, and properly, against the British. As they will continue to be," he added grimly.

"Where our course may lead us remains to be seen. You'll appreciate the hazards of such a past which at any time may rise to plague our present. But we become again, in fact as well as charter, an American privateer, against English shipping. In our hearts we'll know that we're aboard the *Lively Lady.* But in our heads we are the *Red Savage.*

"I promise you battles. Beyond that, nothing."

They cheered again, to his surprise, then turned with enthusiasm to the work still to be done.

One man was missing. No one had seen Stamford since the previous evening. Mr. Sandys offered a reasonable suggestion.

"He'll have taken advantage of the confusion to slip away, as likely as not to swim to the next island. He'd do anything to get out of work. It's good riddance."

Progress for the next few weeks was steady if not spectacular, as was the continued improvement of Ralph O'Hara. Connie O'Hara blossomed anew, her only complaint the continuing necessity to go about barefoot.

"It's as though I was a rural milkmaid," she sighed. "I kicked off my shoes in that struggle with the sea, and even the smallest in the ship's stores are much too large."

Such dainty feet were certainly those of a great lady, Hubbard reflected. He worked awhile with canvas and awl, then surprised her with a pair of sandals of perfect fit if somewhat lacking as articles of adornment. She eyed them rapturously.

"They're wonderful! But where did you learn to cobble?"

"It's my first attempt," Hubbard confessed. "Usually I whittle or carve."

Most days brought at least one swift, heavy shower, gone almost as quickly as it came, refreshing to sweaty men. There were no prolonged or serious storms.

The O'Haras were able to furnish considerable information as to the islands, but of themselves Hubbard learned little more.

"If you can furnish us passage to some friendly harbor, we will be still deeper in your debt," O'Hara said. "From such a spot, no doubt we'll be able to find our way home."

Home, Ralph had let fall, was a plantation. But where it was located, or of its size or prosperity – or very possible poverty – they said nothing.

Refloated with a clean bottom, the *Lively Lady* regained her lost beauty of towering masts and shining fittings, refurbished, her guns warped aboard and emplaced. Water casks were filled, sails set in the last light of a long day. Hubbard intended to waste no time when dawn brought its usual breath of wind.

A cheer went up. He gave no outward sign of disappointment, though he had hoped to get out, to be free of the channels, within sight of the open sea before night closed down. These all but moonless nights were too black to risk so chancy a passage, even should a favoring wind spring up.

To the crew, the restored ship, with work done almost in record time, was a great accomplishment. Hubbard was in full agreement. But his apprehension increased with every hour. Several times each day, for the past week, he had swum across to the rimrocks, climbed to the crest, and stared in half-disbelieving relief at an empty horizon.

But it would not forever remain free of a sail, and any which lifted above these waters was likely to be hostile. If they could make repairs and restore so badly damaged a ship on schedule, then *Calypso* should fare even better in a properly equipped shipyard. The difference of a few days' sailing time, to and from, might be more than compensated by the skill of trained workmen.

At dusk, brief as always like a loosened curtain, there had been only the empty horizon. But a ship or a fleet might creep behind the shelter of the neighboring island. Also a vessel could cover a lot of miles in a night, given a breath of breeze for her sails.

Awakening several times during the night, perhaps because of the more cramped quarters by comparison with the wide luxury of the open beach, Hubbard was uncomfortably conscious that it was not a night of calm. In this sheltered bay the breeze scarcely ruffled the water, but outside there was wind.

A final inspection at dawn was reassuring. There was nothing to see. Back on board, before ducking below to don dry clothes, he nodded to Sullivan, as ready as the eager crew.

"Whenever you're ready." Hubbard felt the stir and quiver as the *Lady* began to move, as he reached his cabin.

Prowling the widening channel there was a new sense of liveliness as the wind came fairly. Hubbard drew his first full breath as they crept out, to round the bigger island and not discover an enemy lurking and ready.

This time there was no cheer. At this stage, the men were taking it for granted.

Finicky and uncertain in these latitudes, the wind fell, leaving them adrift. That it would probably show no more favor to other possible sails was no real comfort. Hubbard preferred to be well away from land when he sighted others.

A fluky wind returned ahead of the dark, but it was fitful and unpredictable. They made slow progress, and Hubbard, as wakeful as on the previous night, sighed with relief as the moon seemed to rise out of the sea. Sullivan eyed him sympathetically.

"It has been rather a strain, these last hours," he observed.

"I'm jumpy as a sack full of oats," Hubbard confessed. "Somehow I've a feeling –"

He broke off. There was nothing to see, still he was certain that he'd glimpsed a patch of white, faint and small with distance. He scrambled to the main stays, surprising the lookout by his sudden advent alongside. To his urgent question, the latter was bewildered.

"Why no, sir, I've made out nothing –"

He broke off, and Hubbard had seen also, the patch of white at the edge of the horizon, slightly clearer, larger than before. The distant lift of a sail, as on that other occasion, newly free of the Sound, when Captain Sir Harry Dupont and his *Indefatigable* had come plunging down at them. He hadn't known the name of her commander at that time, but in the hours which had followed he'd learned something of the seamanship as well as the tenacity of Mad Josh's rival captain.

Now it was he who commanded a different *Red Savage*, but the excitement was the same. Returning to the deck, whence the occasional glimpses were easily visible, he met Sullivan's question with a shrug.

"We'll hold our course. If it should chance to be *Calypso*, and she sights us in turn –"

As undoubtedly she would already have done. He left the thought unfinished. There was no need to elaborate.

Tonight the waxing moon cast light like bread upon the waters, and the sudden veering of the other vessel, its hull able to be glimpsed, testified that it was equally anxious concerning them. A shout from the lookout was scarcely restrained in its excitement.

"Another sail – three points off her starboard!"

Hubbard scrambled aloft a second time,

more breathless than he liked to admit. *Calypso*, if it should be she, or another British man o' war, he would hold steady against and see what might come. But he'd had the feeling all along that *Calypso* would be returning by now, and might well have enlisted the support of a second vessel, to make as certain as possible in a fresh encounter. Vane-Templeton would have learned caution from the savage pounding his vessel had taken at that prior meeting.

As the first ship took on substance he confirmed what had been more certainty than guess. It had had to be the *Calypso*, hurrying at all speed to a second rendezvous, and *Calypso* it was. Having viewed her before at close range, even with repairs and fresh rigging she was unmistakable.

Hubbard became aware of Constance O'Hara beside him, fairy-like in the half-light, dressed in something white. Made free of the stores of the *Lively Lady*, she had found reasonably suitable material and made dresses, showing as much skill with the needle as at make-up and disguise.

"I couldn't sleep," she explained. "I take it that we may be in for a fight?"

The second vessel had also altered course, and that was significant.

"There's the possibility," Hubbard
213

acknowledged. "The nearer ship is *Calypso*."

"Then we will fight?"

Hubbard cast an eye at the sky. A cloud drifted between sea and moon. More were in the offing.

He doubted that storm portended, but an overcast sky changed the complexion. His reply held a note of ambiguity.

"I'd hate for anything to happen before we can set you and Ralph ashore. You've already had a deal of trouble."

Her smile was quick and warm.

"Don't let that influence you, Captain. It won't bother us."

Nor would it, he was sure. Like anyone aboard, including himself, there would be a certain apprehension, an uncomfortable tightening of stomach muscles at the imminence of battle. But that was neither abject fear nor terror.

"That's but one part of it," he confessed. "*Calypso* by herself is one thing. But against two – we'll fight if necessary, but I prefer to be a bit choosy. There's small profit in being battered and sunk, when the odds are against inflicting much damage in turn. As for that other –"

Something about the intruder, distant as she was, gave him his answer. Not only

214

had he seen her more than once at close quarters, he'd stood upon her deck.

More ponderous, immeasurbly more powerful than her consort, she had equal reason to sink them. *Calypso*'s captain had had the luck to engage the support of Sir Harry Dupont and his *Indefatigable*.

TWENTY-SEVEN

Hubbard watched a moment longer, calculating their chances. If the English captains had not yet made sure as to their identity, that would soon come, followed by an engagement if they could bring it about. Sir Harry, outraged at events in and around Plymouth, if permitted to follow his own bent, would have sailed from there in hot quest of them. Whether chance or skill had rewarded him, Captain Vane-Templeton had been able to furnish him the information he craved.

This coming day could be long, or short. Hubbard tingled with eagerness to engage this particular pair, probably as strong as their desire to sink him. But when they fought it would be on his terms. Out here there was wind, along with sea room, and the *Lively*

Lady, rejuvenated, was living up to her name.

He was aware of the disappointment of the crew as they led the chase, men as eager as himself to settle accounts with these others, but there was no grumbling. They had a healthy respect for the power arrayed against them.

Chance or luck might still decide the issue, but short of that they held their distance handily, then a cheer went up as it became clear that by crowding on additional sail they could lose the others if they wished. Hubbard was content to hold his lead without increasing it. With a bit of luck they might fight on his terms, and this account was overdue for a settling.

Land was a darker blotch, distant on the horizon.

Connie and Ralph O'Hara watched from nearby, with as lively an interest in the outcome as any. The girl's uncovered head allowed her hair to ruffle to the breeze, and her face was animated. Ralph gestured as Hubbard joined them.

"I suppose you realize, Captain, that you're heading toward Martinique?"

"No, I hadn't known that," Hubbard confessed, and understood the dilemma which a closer approach might present. During the continuous struggle with

Napoleon, the British had conquered and imposed their rule on most of the West Indies, except for Spanish possessions. That included Martinique, Guadeloupe and small dependencies, once French.

Sovereignty in times such as these was uncertain. Haiti maintained neutrality, but on a precarious basis. She would not welcome an American privateer or be inclined to afford her protection, especially with British ships in hot pursuit. As for the Spanish isles, Spain was allied with England, though not at war with the United States. A game of hide and seek in such waters was fraught with perils and problems peculiar to the islands.

Such information was interesting, but Hubbard was prepared to play his own game, and hazards might be turned to assets. Daylight showed the land more clearly, though still distant. Hubbard ordered breakfast prepared and served, and set the example by dining leisurely with his guests. The relative position of all three ships remained unchanged. With true bulldog spirit, the British were holding on, hoping for a break.

The sun climbed, hung, and commenced its long fall to the sea. The afternoon was wearing on. Hubbard checked his calculations. By nightfall they should be reasonably close to the long reach of Martinique. That would give an excellent opportunity for escape if he wished. But such a maneuver might backfire, forcing an encounter at point-blank range.

He had other plans. Hopefully he could use the covering dark to cut out a single foe, then come upon it suddenly with the advent of the moon. Since his rival captains would be aware of such a possibility, they would be alert, but the odds, with a faster ship properly handled, would be with him.

Hubbard ordered the guns run out, to be ready for action or guard against surprise. Darkfall was swift and heavy, with scant light from the remote stars. The distant land seemed swallowed by the sea.

Hubbard forced himself to an air of indifference he was far from feeling, going below for a couple of hours' sleep. That was safe enough, and it was prudent to be rested and alert by the time the moon should return.

Habit paid off. He slept.

An increasing glow, like a fire barely kindled, was at the eastern edge of the horizon when he returned to the deck. Sullivan had nothing to report. The *Lively Lady*, under half sail, glided almost noiselessly, the breeze putting no strain on her rigging. The strain lay in anticipation, of what the moon might reveal when it burst almost as suddenly as the sun

218

above the horizon. There was the likelihood that it would show an empty sea. Against that was the possibility that both *Indefatigable* and *Calypso* would be close upon them.

He could sense the same strained eagerness in the crew, every man at his station, awaiting what the pulling back of the curtain might bring.

Light came streamingly. A tropic moon, especially as it neared the full, seemed by night little less brilliant than the sun by day.

A vast shadow loomed mountainously. It would be the land mass, closer than they had expected, though Sullivan had been taking soundings for the past hour. But even in deep waters there were risks, not only of running dangerously close but from unknown obstructions.

They had avoided those, but the other and greater nightmare was a near thing. Hubbard, the first to glimpse the heavier outline, knew it for the *Indefatigable*, and their watch was equally good. The seventy-four was between them and the open sea, already commencing to alter course, hopefully to come at them before they could take evasive action.

The lookout, hoarse from excitement, strove to shout a warning while keeping his voice as nearly inaudible as possible. A second sail seemed almost to leap from

219

the dissipating night, moving to hem them in.

Hubbard's calculations were equally fast. *Calypso* was doing her best, and she might be able to come up before the battle was concluded, especially should the *Lively Lady* be staggered and slowed by a well-aimed broadside from the *Indefatigable*. Otherwise, however eager, she must remain a spectator.

Hemmed by land on one side, by Sir Harry's big ship on the other, *Calypso* planned to cut off any chance at retreat. Chance in the night had favored them.

Hubbard gave his orders quietly, and men swarmed aloft, crowding on more sail. The breeze, which had all but died away, was freshening. Hubbard felt the increasing surge, heard a snatch of baffled frustration from the other deck as Sir Harry, trying to match the turn, was caught aback, losing precious headway.

Whatever the result, it would be a near thing. The gravest danger was suddenly the higher loom of the land. Behind such a rise of headlands the wind might be cut off, leaving them becalmed while their enemies, farther out, retained steerageway. It was a gamble of odds. Should it come to a slugging match

220

while they lay helpless, all the advantage would rest with the British.

And it was a fair bet that nothing in his long career would afford Captain Dupont greater pleasure than to pound this particular foe into wreckage.

So far, the wind was holding, even strengthening. The *Lady* showed her liveliness almost with disdain. A ragged cheer went up from the hands, as swiftly silenced at Hubbard's bawled order. But they were drawing ahead.

Which left them by no means free of the trap. The advantage was as temporary as Hubbard had foreseen. Sir Harry was piling on every possible stitch of sail, and under favoring conditions *Indefatigable* was no slouch. Her guns quested, over-eager, but testing. Hubbard's breath eased as splashes fell astern, almost close enough to shower them but short. They were out of range, holding their own. *Calypso* came scudding frantically in their wake, the jaws of the trap having closed too late. Now the dark shoreline seemed to be doing the running, the ships standing still.

Hubbard's hope to lose one of the pair in the night, then engage the other on more even terms, had failed. He could still battle Sir Harry, one to one, but his own ship lacked the smashing power of the seventy-four. The *Lively Lady* had eighteen carronades, each of which fired a thirty-two pound missile. Such a disparity presented problems.

The sensible course would be to hold on, to weather Martinique, refusing an engagement which could so easily prove disastrous. But he had decided at the start to fight, maneuvering for a possible advantage. It might be better to carry the battle to the enemy, to go about suddenly and plunge at *Indefatigable*, firing a broadside, to close and board. Desperate though the maneuver, its surprise might turn the tables.

His hope that Sir Harry would burn more powder, providing a brief leeway for attack, had dwindled. Dupont was too old a hand for useless theatrics.

The mountains rearing alongside were assuming a heavier solidity, the sun silvering the water, dwarfing the hitherto brilliant moon. A great bald crown of mountain loomed in the distance. That would be Pelee, Hubbard decided. Under normal conditions he would view this harbor with appreciation as well as lively curiosity.

The great hills cast their shadows far out, while the land turned from black to the tropic richness of greens. Now there was a rising smoke, drifting like light fog, signs of settlement. To the starboard loomed a bay, a rocky pyramid of mountain lifted at the sky. Ralph O'Hara was alongside.

"Diamond Rock," he said. "Along with Fort-de-France. You'll go far to find a prettier sight."

In the bay and out beyond were the loom of colored sails, fishing boats returning with their catch. The white roofs and walls of Fort-de-France seemed painted against the background. Those aboard the smacks, as well as in the town, would be afforded an excellent view of the impending battle. Though he hadn't planned it with so many interested spectators in mind, it had to be here and now. Either that or make what to their eyes would be an ignominious scud for safety.

There was that temptation, to fight another day on more even terms. Beyond Mont Pelee loomed Cape St. Martin. He could weather the course by holding steady, then, through the straits, shake off pursuit and vanish in the open sea. Moreover there was Connie O'Hara to think of – he'd promised to set her safely ashore somewhere. If the *Lively Lady* went down, the odds were that all aboard would go with her.

All at once the wind was veering, threatening to tack. It might shift or drop, removing whatever advantage he hoped to wring. To make him pay the price of tardiness.

Hubbard cursed himself and opened his mouth to give the order, to come about suddenly while loosing their broadside. Then he swore in fresh incredulity, jaw dropping.

Standing toward Diamond Head, skittering on a course clearly intended to intercept them, came a fresh sail – a sloop, snowy as the distant houses, brave with gilt and gold. She was tearing along at a great rate, something which had the look of a white flag but just as certainly could not be, standing stiff in the breeze. She came cutting with abandoned madness between the *Lively Lady* and the *Indefatigable*, forcing the Britisher to luff suddenly to avoid running her down. Hubbard swore a third time, astonished beyond speech.

TWENTY-EIGHT

It was utterly, completely incongruous, recklessly daring or totally foolhardy, action without precedent, a tiny sloop interposing herself between ships of war already clearing for action. A single well-placed – or misplaced

– shot from either, could blow her out of the water. But she sailed as intrepidly as Daniel braving the lions, pulling up with a smart show of seamanship which Hubbard could not but admire.

For the moment it was impossible to pursue his own intention, to hurtle at *Indefatigable* and engage. This banty rooster was squarely between, with a brazen show of authority which Hubbard could find nothing to justify. He studied her flag again, and was no more enlightened. White it certainly was, but it could hardly be a flag of surrender, or even of truce –

A splotch of yellow, perhaps gold, showed against the white. He turned to Sullivan, watching with equal mystification.

"What do you make of it, Mr. Sullivan?"

Sullivan shook his head.

"I've spent a fair number of years at sea, sir, but I've never beheld the like. She can hardly be Portugee –"

O'Hara was equally mystified. But for the moment the newcomers' attention was for the British. Her decks were cleared for action, though by comparison her guns would be virtually toys. Officers in blue and gold on her deck added an extra touch of color. One bellowed something at *Indefatigable*, as they came up almost under her bows. Forced to lose leeway, Hubbard could picture Sir Harry's almost dancing rage at such interference.

This was the moment, if he cared to take advantage of it, to put enough distance between to avoid any possibility of engagement, but Hubbard was of no more mind for that than before. The intrepid little stranger seemed to feel that she, not they, was in command of the situation.

"What the devil is he about?" Sullivan wondered.

"Square away. We'll go around and see," Hubbard instructed.

He was equally mystified, but the sloop – he could now make her name out, but could not read it, since it was French – had come out from the harbor, and that was just as bewildering. Why should a French vessel, an easy prey, risk being gobbled up by a big Britisher? But a couple of officers were going aboard the *Indefatigable,* and if Captain Sir Harry Dupont would defer to that extent, he could do no less.

"Lower my boat," he instructed. "I'll risk a call on Sir Harry again – under the circumstances. Stand ready for action at a moment's notice," he added to Sullivan, and, requesting Ralph O'Hara to accompany him, was rowed across.

That something as out of the ordinary as unusual was taking place was manifest from the reaction of the Britishers. *Calypso* had pulled up, some distance back, clearly as puzzled as any. The conduct now accorded by Dupont indicated the latter's mystified uncertainty. Along with O'Hara, Hubbard was courteously assisted in an ascent to the deck, though with none of the courtesies normally accorded a visiting captain. That, of course, was not to be expected. He was self-invited, and they were at war, even though some sort of temporary truce was being imposed.

Sir Harry, looking at once baffled and angry, was the center of a little group of his own officers and those who had come from the sloop. He stared an instant at Hubbard, with no great surprise. It was reasonable that he would know who commanded *Red Savage*, and had adjusted his mind to realities.

One of the visitors from the sloop, and the man clearly in charge, was cause for surprise on Hubbard's part. He advanced with hand outstretched, a smiling gesture of welcome, though his fellow-officer glowered, viewing Hubbard askance. Hubbard returned the stare in blank surprise.

The last time he had seen the Marquis d'Ernee was at the latter's estate out from

Plymouth, and though he had viewed him, d'Ernee had not seen him since that parting as they had been about to embark from Connecticut for England, ten years before.

Today, the Marquis was smartly uniformed and attired, wearing ribbons and decorations along with an air of easy authority which was increasingly bewildering. His welcome was cordial.

"Captain Hubbard! This is a genuine pleasure, to renew acquaintance after so long a lapse!"

Though bemused, Hubbard returned the handclasp with equal warmth.

"It's a pleasure, but one I had not expected," he managed.

Sir Harry stood stiff and uncompromising on his own deck, clearly enraged as well as baffled, an emotion in no way lessened as the Marquis showed himself clearly in charge. He half-turned, courteously encompassing the Captain in his smile.

"Captain Hubbard and I are long-time acquaintances," he explained. "And am I correct in my understanding that you have met before?"

Sir Harry unbent enough for a curt nod.

"After a fashion. The last time he was upon my deck he was a – a –"

He checked, on the sudden realization that

to proclaim that Hubbard had been not merely a prisoner but a victim of his press gang, would not sound very well. While everyone knew and understood the reality, impressment was neither discussed nor officially admitted.

"We have met. You show damned cheeky, sir, coming uninvited to my ship, in the face of – of –"

"Of the sparring in which we have been indulging, Sir Harry? I grant you that. But after being signaled to lie to, and then a gathering here which might afford some explanation –" he swung back to d'Ernee.

"If you'll pardon me, sir, I'm more than curious as to what this is all about. Exactly who do you represent, and by what authority do you presume to place yourself between our ships, to interfere with affairs so strictly our own?"

"Yes, b'gad, that's what I want to know," Dupont interjected, then reddened at finding himself in alliance, however temporary, with an enemy shipmaster.

The Marquis spread his hands in a gesture unmistakably French, and deprecatory.

"Surely, Gentlemen, it requires no explanation!" His eyebrows arched. "Or were you both so preoccupied with such matters as to have overlooked the obvious, that here you sail within French territorial waters? So that your actions are an infringement of His Most Christian Majesty's neutrality?"

"Neutrality?" Hubbard echoed. "His Most Christian Majesty?"

The sudden paling of Sir Harry's cheeks showed that he was beginning to understand, but Hubbard was baffled. The Marquis explained.

"You have not heard, Captain Hubbard? But surely, you must recognize the colors of Imperial France? The flag of His Most Christian Majesty, King Louis?"

Hubbard was beginning to get the picture.

"King Louis? Are you telling me that Napoleon has been defeated – that Martinique and these other islands are French again, but under King Louis? That – that your flag is that of the Bourbons?"

The Marquis was still smiling, with a keen appreciation for the ironies of the situation.

"Precisely, Captain Hubbard. France and England are no longer at war. As to the strife between America and England, as a neutral and friend to both of you gentlemen and your countries, I deplore it. But France is officially neutral. As Governor of Martinique, it was impossible for me to sit idly by and permit a hostile engagement to be fought within French territorial waters. You apprehend."

Hubbard was beginning to understand, though coming so suddenly it was a large order. Napoleon fallen, the former monarchy restored! But England and the United States were unaffected in their struggle by such turns, and the only certain result which he could envision, aside from the abrupt termination of the battle which he had been set to begin, would be that England would no longer need to resort to the press gang to secure a full complement of sailors for her ships. With the French and most other navies of the world neutralized, she would have a surplus of both men and vessels, with increased power to hurl against the United States, suddenly standing alone.

Precarious as their situation had been before, this could render it immeasurably worse.

All of which was reason for careful thought and action on his part. He could not afford to sacrifice the *Lively Lady* without exacting as much damage in turn as his best efforts might devise.

He sorted out another puzzling piece of information for clarification.

"And you say, sir, that you are now the French Governor, in these waters?"

The Marquis understood the full implications of the question.

"I have been granted that honor. Permit me, Captain Dupont, to enlighten him upon matters which are sufficiently strange. You are familiar, I believe, with the abduction of my daughter – of Renee –"

His voice caught. Then, regaining command of himself, he went on smoothly.

"It quickly became apparent how outlandishly Poynter had tricked us, abducting Renee and Robert, sailing away with them. You will understand how frantic was their mother and myself. It seemed providential that almost at once I should be proffered the Governorship here of Martinique, since we had reason to suppose that Poynter might head for the Indies as the only possible sanctuary open to him. From here I hoped for a closer base of operations, hopefully to effect a rescue.

"We made a swift passage, and not long after, were doubly favored by good fortune. Renee, Robert, their personal servants and a sailor, put in to this very harbor, all unharmed. They have told me of your captivity along with them on the same ship, of your kindness –"

His voice faltered, then he recovered and went on.

"Also of the battle in which they managed

to escape from the ship. That was Robert's idea, and of an extreme rashness, though I concede that they feared for their lives, terrified to remain within the power of that scoundrel. Fortunately, luck favored them. Renee and Robert are safe at home with their mother and myself. She will –"

He checked, at the realization that he was allowing his pleasure to carry him away. He bowed formally to Sir Harry.

"I am sure that she will be more pleased to have both you gentlemen pay your respects, while in harbor. It is a fortuitous streak of fortune which permits it."

Sir Harry heard him with clearly mixed emotions, then sputtered an immediate protest.

"I fear that under the stress of excitement I overlooked how close we were venturing to the shore, thus straying into French territorial waters," he admitted. "It was an inadvertent error which I regret. As I am sure is the case with Captain Hubbard also. But it is a mistake which we will rectify with all possible despatch, betaking ourselves and our vessels back to the open sea." He inclined his head slightly to Hubbard.

"As for partaking of your hospitality, my dear Marquis, or rendering my homage to the Lady Renee, I regret that the duty upon

233

which I am engaged must come first. So I fear that will have to await a more auspicious occasion."

"And much as I'm delighted at the news of her good health and restoration to the bosom of her family, I must concur with Captain Dupont," Hubbard added. "The neutrality of France does not affect the struggle between our countries. Being at war, we are obliged to continue. Certainly we will take ourselves well away from territorial waters, without delay," mounting anew at what he could not but regard as effrontery. British might had restored these possessions to the French, and placed Louis XVIII again on his throne. In return, France should show a proper appreciation. "Almost I would regard this as an unwar –"

Belatedly recollecting his position, he choked down the words. But his duty as a captain in the navy clearly weighed heavier with him than to pay his respects to a woman – one who had been less than anxious to receive him when he had sought her at her home in England.

Hubbard, though eager to see Renee again, was with Sir Harry in this. Assured that she was safe, he could fight with an easier conscience, even though the possible consequences chilled him as they had not done only minutes before. If he should *not* see her again –

The Marquis was suddenly stern, coldly implacable.

"You gentlemen are forgetting, I think," he reminded them. "Not only can I permit no fighting within French territorial waters, but there is also the twenty-four hour rule – one which, I fear, has been so long neglected as to be almost forgotten. But it remains entirely valid, and must be enforced. Your ships, all three of them, must put in to the harbor, and remain there for that period of time."

Dupont's dismayed glance met Hubbard's, clearly as startled by that overlooked rule. Hubbard's mind raced beyond the twenty-four hour limit, prescribed for just such cases, to what might then ensue. At its expiration, a situation would result almost certain to be more profitable to the British than himself, with two ships to his one and time in which to plan and maneuver.

For, part and parcel of the rule, was the proviso that the ships of hostile navies might not depart together, even at the expiration of the twenty-four hour grace period. One or the other could leave, but the rival vessel must wait an added day.

Ample time for the one which went first to make good its escape – or to position itself just beyond the territorial limit and be set to sink its rival before it could get into position to retaliate.

Aside from the prospect of seeing Renee in the interval, Hubbard liked no part of it. Nor, as certainly, did Sir Harry.

"Damn it, sir," Dupont roared. "I regard this as an unwarrantable interference with the sovereign rights of England. To say nothing of – of others."

The Governor remained coldly correct.

"These articles, Sir Harry, were entered into by the leading maritime powers, including your own."

Dupont was not placated.

"Forgotten rules," he snorted. "What's to stop us from sailing ahead and resuming our own business?"

"My authority, sir," d'Ernee reminded him, his tone suddenly cold. "I represent the Majesty of France –"

"Damn t´–" Sir Harry bit off his words. They would be peculiarly insulting, and those in higher places might not take kindly to his interference in affairs of state. "You might close your eyes for just a few minutes,". he added in weak amendment.

"I did not hear what you said, Sir Harry," the Marquis returned, again smiling, then was stony. He gestured.

"The guns of my small ship entail no threat to such vessels as yours. But the guns of Fort Bourbon, on the heights yonder, along with those of Trois-Ilets – there are a score of them, trained on us at this moment. Thirty-two pounders, Gentlemen. I am sure you understand."

TWENTY-NINE

Sir Harry eyed d'Ernee with a new and grudging respect. Until then, in his mind the father of his intended bride had seemed little more than a twig off the foppish French tree of decayed aristocracy, to be brushed aside rather than taken seriously.

Hubbard had made no such error. The Marquis was a man as well as a governor, aware both of his privileges and responsibilities; and as he had pointed out, fully capable of enforcing his orders.

Thirty-two pounders were vastly more damaging than twenty pounders. No ship could long survive their fire, and all three vessels were like sitting ducks on a pond, under those invisible but almost omnipotent guns. That the Marquis, as Governor and representative of his King, would at need implement his threat, was only too plain.

Dupont swung on Hubbard in fresh rage.

"You knew about this, and ran for their shelter," he charged.

Hubbard all but choked. "I knew nothing of them," he snapped. "I'd like nothing better than to take you both on," he added with a gesture toward the *Calypso*, and in his sudden heat he meant it.

Dupont checked at the Marquis' reminder. "Gentlemen, remember the rule. Twenty-four hours."

He went on to refresh their memory. "At the expiration of that period, one of you may leave, but not both. A full day and night must elapse between times of departure. As representative of His Most Christian Majesty, I am required to enforce the rule."

He was within not only his rights but his duty. Forgetful of all but forgotten rules, Hubbard and Dupont alike had allowed themselves to be trapped. Hubbard shrugged his acceptance. But Sir Harry was driven almost to frenzy.

"You'd like nothing better than to go out first!" he charged. "Good God! A twenty-four hour start! *I'll* go first."

"Over my dead body," Hubbard returned grimly. "Since I was first in, it's only proper

238

that I should be the first out." But he was equally appalled. To sail into such a trap, be bottled up, then to allow the enemy to withdraw and take up position to intercept and sink him as he emerged – that was unthinkable.

But they were both in the same fix. Sir Harry's career must come to a bitter conclusion if he allowed such a thing to happen, and the news reached the Admiralty. It was impasse, but with the gravest implications.

Then the irony of it struck Hubbard, and he exploded with laughter. Sir Harry scowled, affronted.

"I'm damned if I can perceive the humor," he grunted.

"It's as easy to laugh as cry," Hubbard returned. "Washington would look upon this from a point of view very similar to London's, I'm afraid. But it seems to be out of our hands, at least for the present."

The Marquis intervened.

"That, Gentlemen, is precisely what I mean. The situation seems to have, shall I say, crept up on all of us? None of us intended it, but we are faced with reality. But if I might offer a suggestion? Why not anchor in Fort-de-France, at least overnight? All three of you. Perhaps with consideration the situation may be resolved. In any case, nothing beyond a few hours will be lost, the situation will remain as before. And for your ships to lie hove to on a lee shore is not the best of seamanship."

Hubbard could see that Sir Harry was tempted. The *Lively Lady* had casks full of fresh water, as was undoubtedly the case with *Calypso*, but *Indefatigable* had probably been longer at sea and could profit by an opportunity to secure fresh provisions. And a brief break would give no more advantage to one side than the other.

"I am happy to see you gentlemen in agreement, at least on this point," the Marquis took prompt advantage. "Also it gives me great pleasure to extend my personal invitation to you both, along with the captain of *Calypso*, to come ashore during the afternoon, quite informally of course, to tender your respects to my Countess and to our daughter, the Lady Renee. Both would be devastated at anything less."

He was showing them a marked courtesy, though under the circumstances that too amounted to a command. Because of the unusual nature of the circumstances, he was being as informal as possible.

They bowed acceptance, hesitated a moment, then nodded jerkily to each other. Again the Marquis solved the touchy question of preference.

"Since these waters are under French jurisdiction, you will permit, Sir Harry, that I assume temporarily the role of host?" He bowed to Hubbard. "It has been a genuine pleasure to renew old acquaintance, Captain."

Thus escorted to the side, Hubbard descended to his waiting boat. He had been greatly daring in going uninvited to such a conference on his enemy's vessel, but it had seemed necessary, and he doubted if protocol had ever envisaged such a particular situation. His mind was filled with a myriad of matters as he was piped aboard the *Lively Lady*, and they proceeded sedately to an anchorage. Eventually, the problem of escape from the harbor must be decided, followed by the postponed battle. This could be but an interlude.

Following the twenty-four hour limit, either he or the British would be at liberty to up anchor and depart at any time, at least in theory. Practice was another matter entirely. They could not go together, since that would violate the rule, and he certainly would not sit idly by and permit his enemy to secure such an advantage. Just as surely, Dupont and Vane-Templeton would be on guard against any such attempt on his part.

But for the remainder of that day, in full daylight and under the guns of the forts, neither would risk such folly or breach of hospitality. Which left him the chance to accept the invitation and see Renee again! Renee!

He had scarcely had time to think about all that he had heard, how that desperate escape from the *Lively Lady* and the unwelcome durance imposed by Poynter had resulted; the fact that she was here, alive and well – and probably as eager and excited as himself.

Even should an opportunity present itself to slip away, doing so without seeing her again, he would pass it up. Renee came first. Fortunately, no such test between duty and devotion would be imposed.

He scowled at the reflection that Sir Harry would be calling also, to pay his respects, while chafing with an added fury of jealousy. Well, they'd still be on neutral ground, but there was no question in his mind as to whom Renee would be most pleased to welcome.

He checked at sight of Constance O'Hara, looking cool and comfortable despite the increasing heat, gazing eagerly toward the shore. That part was a welcome dividend. She and her brother could be set ashore in the best possible of ports, their tribulations at an end.

They were ready to go, the small store of dunnage which they had accumulated packed.

"It's not that we're anxious to be quit of the *Red Savage*, Captain, or of your hospitality," Constance assured him, and her hand, resting against his palm, was cool yet warm. "We owe a debt of gratitude, one beyond our ability to pay. But the opportunity to do a bit of shopping, after all these months – I'm looking forward to that."

"That is more than easy to understand." Hubbard was suddenly diffident. "If I could perhaps advance you folks such monies as you may require, until you can get in touch with friends or business associates –"

"We are deeply appreciative," Ralph assured him. "But that will not be necessary. We are known here, and such arrangements will be readily taken care of."

He despatched them in a boat to the shore. Only the thought of seeing Renee again made the leave-taking easy. A very real friendship had developed between the three of them. Well, some day they might meet again. After the strangeness of encounters in which he had participated, almost anything was possible.

Later, freshly shaven, attired in the best captain's uniform to which he had fallen heir along with command of the *Lively Lady*, he had himself set ashore and began the walk up from the quay to the governor's mansion. The sun blazed white-hot, and it occurred to him that custom as well as the heat of the afternoon might have decreed waiting until evening. But he had been sweating with eagerness for hours.

The gleaming white mansion, flanked by cool greenery, showed temptingly inviting. A colored footman, brave in a smart livery and with carefully powdered hair, welcomed him and departed to announce him. With a flash of annoyance, Hubbard remembered that his own hair was unpowdered. It required some thought to recall the last time that he had indulged in such frippery. That civilized beings still indulged in such practices had totally slipped his mind.

The spacious anteroom was relatively cool, opening upon another room to the side. Through it came the murmur of voices. Glancing with more than a touch of expectation, he stared, amazed. However great his eagerness, his impatience to be here, others had been ahead.

Captain Sir Harry Dupont, brave in

elaborate dress, a sword by his side, was bowing over the white fingers of a lady, staring up at her face as one bemused. The lady, surprisingly enough under the circumstances, was not Renee. To Hubbard's increasing bewilderment, she was Constance O'Hara, whose shopping appeared to have been amply rewarded. Attired in a soft pastel of shimmering gray silk, with accessories to match, she was every inch the great lady, as ravishingly beautiful as a dream.

THIRTY

Dupont, of course, had come ostensibly at the Governor's invitation, but actually of course to pay his long-deferred respects to Renee. Clearly he had been surprised, and pleasantly so. From the look in his eyes, he would hardly care whether he saw Renee or not.

Hubbard found himself shaking with excitement as he awaited the return of the footman. At the prospect of meeting Renee again he was more moved even than when coming upon her in the arbor out from Plymouth. Though today there was a difference. After a lapse of a decade, he had been uncertain, both of her and himself. Now everything was changed. And yet –

Somehow that day in England seemed incredibly remote and distant. He had been a hunted fugitive. But Renee had been an old friend, the daughter of a fugitive also, long barred from his native land. Now her father was the Governor –

Only one thing was unchanging, constant. His love for Renee, and her's for him. She was suddenly beside him, exclaiming, the half-mischievous gleam in her eyes suffused in a swimming tenderness. But she drew back as he advanced, suddenly shy.

"Not now, Bran," she protested. "This isn't the time, or place! But feeling as I do, it's wonderful to know that you are the same, that you're here, and safe!"

A cough announced the arrival of her father. Bareheaded but bewigged, powdered and faultlessly attired, Hubbard was surprised that d'Ernee looked no older than he had remembered him from the past. Aboard the *Indefatigable*, the Marquis had been hatted and very much the Governor, and there had been no time to notice.

"May I join in welcoming you to Martinique, Captain?" The suspicion of a twinkle in his eyes was matched by the tone of voice. "Not," he added, "that any warmth seems to have been lacking in that already extended."

Renee was in no whit discomposed. "Could I do less than emulate you, Father?" she asked demurely.

"Circumstances place certain strictures upon all of us," the Marquis returned. "Conditions which hopefully may soon be removed. But I assure you, Captain, that my personal welcome is of a matching quality."

He seemed to imply more than he expressed, and Renee gave him a startled glance, then was suddenly in his arms.

"Oh, Father! You *are* a dear."

"Why, so your Mother has sometimes assured me. It gratifies me that you join in the assessment. Shall we go where she awaits us, to add her welcome?"

The Countess welcomed him graciously, extending both her hands in a warm gesture.

"Renee has informed us how, though yourself a prisoner aboard the *Red Savage*, you contrived to save all aboard her from destruction. We are deeply grateful, everlastingly in your debt."

This, Hubbard realized, was both meaningful and a tremendous concession. They were of the nobility, one of the greatest families of France, while he was captain of a privateer, but not much else. Still in the middle of a war, his immediate as well as ultimate prospects were limited. Once his ship was able to put to sea again, he and it were likely to go to the bottom with no waste of time. Those reflections were sobering.

His initial annoyance at finding that, prompt as he had been at availing himself of the Marquis' invitation, both English captains had preceded him, was somewhat dissipated. Eager as he had been, he had restrained himself, with an eye to the proprieties.

Since their vessels were anchored closer to the shore, he had missed seeing them put in. A distant murmur of voices sounded through open French windows. Captain Vane-Templeton strolled beside a lady who looked up to dazzle him with her smile. Closer at hand, Sir Harry still danced attendance on Constance O'Hara, a bewildering vision of loveliness in silks and satins. Noticing his bewilderment, Renee explained.

"Miss O'Hara is no stranger to Fort-de-France, or so I am assured. Mademoiselle Poincard is a particular friend of hers, and, as you may see, much of a size and build, each able to wear the others' clothes – until a selection of outfits may be properly tailored to the needs of Miss O'Hara."

That explained the speed of the

transformation. That Constance was also welcomed as a new arrival from the *Lively Lady* told much more, which neither she nor her brother had bothered to touch upon. Clearly, they possessed both wealth and position.

Both captains were clearly bemused and delighted by such company. Sir Harry, if not completely overwhelmed, was at least distracted from paying more than lip service to Renee.

Confirming his own observation, the Countess was beside him again, following Hubbard's glance with half-amused understanding.

"Perhaps it would be a poor choice of words to suggest that the Captain is sunk, but at least he is impressed. Certainly his attention has been diverted from Renee, much to her relief – and mine. Were you not aware, when adding the O'Haras to your list of rescued, that they are among the great landowners of the islands?"

"They never thought to mention it." He added, a thought maliciously, "Sir Harry has perhaps been faster in such a discovery."

Later, the social aspects of their calls having been consummated, the Marquis, as Governor, brought the three captains together again, this time on neutral ground. His glance from one to another was hopeful rather than expectant.

"I must confess, Gentlemen, that as yet I have been unable to come up with any sort of a solution to the impasse in which you are gripped. Perhaps you have been more successful?"

Vane-Templeton was holding his temper in check with difficulty. Sir Harry was his senior, and he found himself relegated almost to the position of spectator, forced to be an unwilling participant.

"We could settle this nicely between ourselves, if left alone," he growled. "And with every appreciation for your courtesies, Monsieur le Governor, I think it should be left that way."

The Marquis shrugged deprecatingly.

"I am quite in agreement," he said. "Unfortunately, we are all bound by our responsibilities to our respective countries, to the laws of neutrality to which each subscribes – and which I, as Governor of Martinique, have no choice but to enforce. But let us look upon the bright side. War is a tedious business, frequently dull. For all of us, it has lasted overlong. I can scarcely recall when it was not the prevailing condition. Against so timeless a background, what are a few hours, even a few days? We are presented with opportunity for respite, and for you gentlemen, a vacation of sorts. One which all may enjoy with no loss of prestige or advantage. You agree, I hope, that Fort-de-France has many pleasant attributes?"

The Englishmen eyed each other and Hubbard warily. Hubbard was not so circumscribed.

"I find it so," he conceded.

"When you put it that way, Your Excellency, I can say no less," Sir Harry admitted.

His grin made Vane-Templeton seem suddenly boyish.

"There are compensations. Mademoiselle Poincard – a fire-eating Yankee in her sympathies, though she's scarcely set foot off this island. If she could but see London –"

He broke off, coloring. Hubbard found him suddenly likeable.

"Then, for the present at least, why don't we make the best of a not too bad situation?" The Marquis asked. "I know that my wife and daughter – assisted by certain other ladies – are hoping that we may be able to entertain you gentlemen and your officers at a ball. In fact, the entire community looks forward to it with great expectation."

Hubbard saw the sudden animation in the

251

eyes of both. They almost hung on d'Ernee's words.

"Not to impose too great a strain, we will strive to have the ball by tomorrow evening," the Marquis added. "This, of course, is unofficial. You will receive formal invitations in due course."

Vane-Templeton vented his lingering irritation as, following their leave-taking, he and Sir Harry strolled to where their boats awaited them. For the moment, they could speak freely.

"From a purely personal standpoint, I'm looking forward to it," he confessed. "Though I fear I've forgotten how to dance! But as captain of a ship of the royal navy – blast it, Sir Harry, I don't like our situation. This Hubbard is the devil. These Yankees are clever, and there's no guessing what he may come up with."

"I'm sure we can be as alert and at need as clever as any American," Dupont growled. "And my problems are greater than your's. Your crew have had considerable shore-leave, and very recently, while your ship was being refitted. Mine have not only been much longer at sea, but even while at Plymouth, only a few select men could be permitted to set foot on land."

252

"I know. It's the devil of a mess, and worse in that the poor devils see their officers disporting on the beach. Also this is a veritable paradise, far removed from the mainland, so they feel that they should be allowed some freedom."

"But far too big, both as city and island. Too much room in which to scatter and vanish."

"Precisely. But every hour or day they are forced to stay cooped up –"

"My point exactly. Still we can't risk allowing them on shore. But this ball tomorrow night may solve that problem, to a workable extent. I think I see a way to please the men, to afford them a change, with a certain amount of relaxation, and at a minimum of risk."

"If you can, sir, you're a genius. It would certainly help. Their mood verges on the ugly."

Though neither captain voiced the word mutiny, it clearly was much on their minds.

"We'll be ashore tomorrow evening, with our senior officers," Sir Harry went on. "But the juniors can keep an eye on things, with no distress to us. The responsibility will do 'em good. Also, they'd feel left out, otherwise. What I have in mind is a party of sorts aboard *Indefatigable,* since she has greater room. With your crew over – all save a few hands to stand the watch. And perhaps – yes, I think even some guests from the town. They'll have a chance to mingle and exchange gossip – to drink and skylark, not to the extent they'd prefer or manage ashore, but enough to break the monotony. What do you think?"

Vane-Templeton was enthusiastic.

"They'll be drunk and useless for the next day, but that won't matter," he conceded. "Once over their headaches, they'll be properly grateful."

"And Hubbard and his officers will be at the ball, where we can keep an eye on 'em," Sir Harry pointed out. "No chance for Yankee trickery."

THIRTY-ONE

True to the Governor's promise, at mid-morning of the following day a midshipman knocked at Hubbard's cabin. Guessing what it might be, Hubbard welcomed the interruption. He was laboriously bringing his log up to date, a distasteful chore at all times and doubly so now, but necessary.

That Denny Poynter had disdained to be bothered about such matters rendered it even more imperative. The pounding to which the *Lively Lady* had been subjected might account for the *Red Savage*'s past records, but current ones were almost certain to be required, at some future date.

There was a letter, sealed on the back with an elaborate coat of arms. Even knowing what it contained, he opened it with mounting excitement. For the promised ball, he cared nothing. Had it been possible, he would have avoided it. Social affairs with pomp and glitter dismayed him, despite the training which he had received as a petty officer, grimly supervised by unwilling seniors. But Renee would be there. That made all the difference.

Dated from the Governor's House, formally couched, the invitation was from His Excellency and His Countess, requesting the pleasure of Captain Bransom Hubbard and his lieutenants that evening, at eight o'clock.

A single word added that there would be dancing.

Such a ball, attended by the important ladies and gentlemen of the island, might offer embarrassments to rival officers, but at least the ice had been broken. This was the epitome of courtesy. But with it arose fresh problems.

There was still the unsolved matter of which of the rival ships should be permitted to sail out from the harbor, past the guns of the forts, thus gaining that vital twenty-four advantage. Lying sleepless, Hubbard had pondered anew, to no avail. Any sudden dash for freedom, on the part of any of the three, could and would be countered. As Governor, the Marquis had made abundantly clear that he would not hesitate at doing his duty.

Hubbard's junior officers – Mr. Sullivan, Mr. Sandys and Mr. Richter, were in a flurry of excited preparation. It had been a long while since they had attended any sort of party, to say nothing of a Governor's Ball. Americans though they were, they felt a certain awe of nobility such as the Marquis d'Ernee and Sir Harry Dupont. Sir Harry was English and an enemy, still he would be a fellow-guest. And there would be ladies – island beauties, probably by the dozen if not the score.

It was Hubbard, coming on deck, the first to be ready, who noticed the procession of laden boats, moving from *Calypso* across to her bigger neighbor, returning empty and at speed to take on fresh loads.

For a moment he stared, puzzled, his thoughts jumping suspiciously to the possibility that his rival captains had between them concocted some plan for his humiliation. Then, studying the others closely through the glass, observing their manifest excitement, he understood.

For himself, he was keeping his crew to ship, allowing no shore leave, at least not at this stage of their visit. He would have far less to fear from desertion than either Sir Harry or Vane-Templeton, but another possibility, however remote, had decided him against it. Should any opportunity present itself for slipping out from the harbor under cover of darkness, stealing a march on the enemy, he wanted his crew at hand, instantly ready. In any case, they had enjoyed weeks of shore leave on an island, and recently.

The British, not daring to trust their crews ashore, but fearing at least a threat of mutiny as they beheld their officers enjoying privileges denied them, were making the most of this opportunity to provide some entertainment. Everyone from both crews would be aboard the *Indefatigable* for the night. And wildly drunk by midnight.

Asleep and sodden by daylight.

Aware of those risks, Sir Harry and Vane-Templeton were taking them, sure that they could keep himself and his officers under their eyes all during the ball; and that with daylight the Governor's edict and the guns of the forts would provide necessary precautions.

Which was only a reasonable assumption, Hubbard admitted dourly. Still, this was a matter of thought.

They were hastening to complete the transfer from *Calypso* to *Indefatigable* before the abrupt onset of darkness, clearly considering that the least of two evils. In any case, what was happening would be known on shore and to the *Red Savage*, and doing it openly would avoid misunderstanding. Also, the presence of Sir Harry Dupont still on his own quarter-deck as the others arrived would have a sobering effect, holding horseplay to proper limits.

But night had fallen when Hubbard's gig grated at the beach and he and his lieutenants stepped ashore. Flaming torches, held by colored servants in resplendent uniforms, lit the quay welcomingly. In the distance, Hubbard was aware of subdued stir, the coming and going of coaches and carriages, a wail of fiddles, the lift of laughter. Again, anxious as he was to see Renee, Hubbard had been determined not to be first.

Apparently the others had been actuated by the same notion. The gigs from *Calypso* and *Indefatigable* were landing their complement of officers at almost the same moment, a little farther along the quay. Crimson

258

reflected from gold epaulettes and fancy buttons. Hubbard glimpsed Vane-Templeton, tugging nervously at his stock, then silence fell on both sides as the rival parties passed within easy hailing distance. No rules of etiquette were provided for such a situation. Hubbard, catching Sir Harry's glance as they approached the open doors, inclined his head. Dupont returned the salutation with equal stiffness.

Lights were everywhere, the sound of music flooding outward. Footmen awaited them, taking charge. The Marquis and his Countess, resplendent, were by the stairs. At her father's left was Renee, and at sight of her, Hubbard forgot all else.

Always, he had known that she was beautiful, desirable, completely winsome. Yet somehow he had not remembered even a half.

The next hour remained a blur. He greeted his host and hostess, introduced his officers, gave back formal bows with the British officers, warmed with appreciation at sight of Constance and Ralph O'Hara; he danced, with a sense of uncertainty, almost of clumsiness, with the Countess, with Renee, then with Constance, afterward with her friend, Miss Poincard. Mirth was not far from the surface in the eyes of all three girls, but there was a deeper, more

259

tender glow in Renee's. All three put him at his ease.

His observation that Sullivan and his other officers, also the English, were initially as stiff and ill at ease lent a measure of reassurance. They were seamen, accustomed to ships and war, not to ballrooms and the arts of peace.

He sighed. England and France, at long last, were at peace. What a pleasure it would be if England and America could compose their differences also!

Despite vagrant thoughts, the evening was delightful, particularly when dancing with Renee in his arms. Her smile, mischievous, as suddenly misty and tender, held the intoxication of wine.

The night was wearing on, so it would soon be expedient to leave, along with his officers. What Sir Harry and Vane-Templeton might do was strictly their business, but undoubtedly they would follow his example, fearing any possible advantage which he might gain if out from under their eye.

A midshipman came obliquely across the floor, striving to hurry and still maintain decorum. Something was exciting the English, throwing them almost into confusion.

"You pardon for the interruption, sir," Mr. Murray said urgently. "But something's afoot –"

He checked as another messenger, clearly from one of the English ships, implored the attention of the Governor. In the sudden startled hush, his words carried clearly.

"Beg to report that *Calypso*'s gone – somehow cut out and no longer in the harbor!"

He added on a breathless note, "No sign of her anywhere, even though the moon's up!"

His reference to the moon was almost as significant, that a ship could have gotten away during the hours of darkness.

Vane-Templeton, as the man most concerned, rushed to a window to peer out. From the Governor's mansion an excellent view of the harbor was outspread.

The others were only an instant behind. The report was accurate. *Indefatigable* lay quietly at anchor, and in the distance the *Lively Lady* seemed to drowse. Vane-Templeton rounded on Hubbard.

"If you're responsible for this –" he began thickly, but was checked by Sir Harry, a hand more rough than placating on his arm.

"Easy, sir," he cautioned. "There's a mystery here, but Captain Hubbard and his officers have been here along with us all evening."

The certainty of that slowed his fellow-captain. A ship might be moved, even slipping out unobserved and unchallenged in the hours of heavy gloom, but it could not sail of its own accord. Even manned by a select crew of boarders – and with only a small watch left on board, a few determined men might have surprised and taken it without causing an alarm – to up-anchor and handle such a vessel would require skilled handling. Junior officers could hardly have managed, nor would a cutting-out expedition of such daring be entrusted to them.

"I give you my word, Captain, that I know nothing of this," Hubbard assured Vane-Templeton. The occasion seemed to call for such reassurance. "You will find my crew and junior officrs on board the *Red Savage*, most of them undoubtedly asleep."

Vane-Templeton's reluctant acknowledgement was an angry shake of the head.

"But it's impossible. Beyond belief."

The Marquis had been questioning some of his servants. He was equally puzzled.

"Apparently no one has seen or heard anything," he observed. That would not be too surprising, with merriment centered both on shore and on the decks of the neighboring *Indefatigable*. "But we'll get to the bottom of this," he added grimly. "My government is concerned with such a breach."

"But it's my ship that's gone," Vane-Templeton protested. The magnitude of the disaster was just beginning to dawn on him. For a captain to lose his ship under any circumstances was sufficiently disastrous. But to explain to an inquiring Admiralty how such a thing might have happened, while he was enjoying himself at a ball on shore –

"I'm ruined," he added under his breath, but followed the others outside. The messengers had been able to add nothing to the stark disclosure which had so abruptly terminated the festivities.

Save that the spot where *Calypso* had anchored was empty, there was no excitement, no sign of any disturbance. Hubbard despatched his officers back to the *Lively Lady*, to make certain that nothing was amiss there. The captains of *Indefatigable* and *Calypso* prepared to return to the former, while the Marquis ordered out a small boat to accompany them to the same destination. He readily acceded to Hubbard's request to go along.

The big seventy-four was surprisingly calm as the small boats came alongside, as though a night of revelry had left everyone too exhausted – or sodden with drink – to be aroused even by such news. The junior officers of both vessels were scrambling to attention, manifestly frightened by a development which they were equally at a loss to understand but feared to be held responsible for.

Hubbard ascended at the heels of the Marquis, again an uninvited guest, but Sir Harry merely glanced at him as he tried to glean something new from his officers. They were equally in the dark. None had seen or heard any disturbance. Only the sudden light of the moon, revealing the emptiness where *Calypso* had rested, had roused a lookout to dazed incredulity.

It was Hubbard, peering over the side into the deep shadows, who detected something not quite as it should be.

"There appears to be a small boat alongside, Captain," he informed Sir Harry. "Fastened in place."

Investigation disclosed four men in the boat, tied and gagged. They had been left as a token watch aboard *Calypso*.

Too cramped and stiff to ascend by themselves, they were hoisted to the deck of the *Indefatigable*, where they managed an explanation of what had happened.

They had been surprised, seized and clubbed unconscious by a sudden rush of boarders. One man had seen and heard enough to make sure that these were from more than one boat, each crowded with pirates.

"How do you know they were pirates?" Vane-Templeton demanded, obviously disbelieving.

"They looked and acted like pirates, sir – and one o' them addressed their leader as Cap'n Poynter. And everybody knows *him* for a pirate!"

THIRTY-TWO

Poynter! Hubbard started with the rest, equally surprised, but only for a moment. So unexpected an attack, daring and well executed, was entirely in keeping. And while he had at first assumed that Denny Poynter had jumped to his death, second thoughts and inquiry had left a measure of doubt.

There were rumors, apparently well-founded, of a cave, invisible from above and nearly so from the sea, somewhere at the water's edge, close below where Poynter had leaped; a cave known to Stamford, the sailor with whom he had several times seen

Poynter in converse, and who had vanished from the *Lively Lady*'s crew and the island at the same time.

Apparently Poynter, learning of the cave, had made particular inquiry as to its location, then had preferred it to a further contest with Hubbard. It might well have contained a hidden boat. Almost certainly, the two had escaped together.

If that was conjecture, it was made plausible by tonight's events. Thirsting for revenge, Stamford had led Poynter to some lair of the Brethren of the Coast, and Poynter had promised them a rich booty under his leadership. With some spying and word of mouth, they had followed the movements of the *Lively Lady*, crammed themselves into a couple of cutters, and descended on Fort-de-France, with the intent of retaking the *Lively Lady*.

To slip into the harbor, under cover of night, led by crew members knowledgeable as to these waters, had been contrived without too much difficulty. The celebrations, ashore and afloat, with even the officers from the forts attending the Governor's ball, had rendered it reasonably simple and easy.

Hubbard could understand the rest. Poynter had probably assumed that shore leave would have been given most of the crew, thus rendering a surprise attack no great risk. But a bit of scouting, along with inquiry in the town, would have shown the hopelessness of any such raid against the *Lively Lady*.

Committed to an enterprise from which there could be no turning back, Poynter as a counter would have learned of the goings-on aboard the *Indefatigable*, along with the virtual desertion of its crew from *Calypso*.

The raiders had been more than willing to substitute *Calypso* for the *Lively Lady*. By now, they were clearly beyond the guns of the forts, standing out to sea.

Vane-Templeton swore savagely as he reached a matching conclusion. The daring of such a feat was lost on him, as was his ship. But Sir Harry was not only practical but swift in reaction.

"Don't worry," he said grimly. "We'll lose no time in pursuit." He remembered to turn to the Marquis. "By your leave, of course, sir."

"Oh, by all means," d'Ernee agreed. "With the understanding that when this episode is determined, you will return to this harbor, with both ships, the provisions of neutrality to resume."

"You have my word for that." At this sign,

Mr. Blastic was already bellowing orders, to call all hands, up anchor, set sail and get under way. The beginning of the dawn breeze was adding itself to such wind as had aided the pirates.

But it proved a task not easy of execution. Not only was *Indefatigable* crowded to a point of confusion with its guests from *Calypso*, but both crews, having celebrated boisterously, were as heavily asleep as Hubbard had anticipated. The frantic efforts of their officers to arouse them were meeting with a sluggish response.

Sir Harry checked impatiently as Hubbard accosted him.

"With your permission, Sir Harry, and yours, Marquis, I'll return to my ship, and join in the chase, subject to the same provisions. But I have a stake in this as well, as all of you gentlemen will perceive. And if you'll pardon my pointing it out, *Calypso* may well manage to outsail the *Indefatigable*. But the *Savage*, with her bottom newly scraped, has at least a matching turn of speed."

Dupont was startled. The suggestion that he should work in alliance with an enemy was more than he had bargained for. Then a wintry amusement flashed in his eyes.

"It's highly irregular, but so is this entire situation. If the Governor has no objections,

I certainly have not. We may have need of your help."

Just how much need became increasingly apparent when, having been rowed back to the *Lively Lady*, finding Mr. Sullivan urgently preparing a rested and eager crew for possible action, Hubbard looked back to the big frigate he had so recently left. A distressfully small crew, revealed in the still half-light, were attempting, without much success, to get some sail on her. But she lay immobile, at the moment far from ready, despite the frantic efforts of both captains and their officers. Just how desperate those would be, Hubbard could picture. This was a further humiliation for British ships, while the American was obviously ready for action.

Hubbard watched a moment, intrigued less by what he saw than by what was not taking place, then gave the order to approach, rather than head for the open sea.

"I've an idea that Poynter has left them another surprise," he observed to Sullivan. "Which would be entirely in keeping."

Denny Poynter had an agile mind, and he was always quick to seize an opportunity. If he could cripple or even temporarily delay the other Britisher from its pursuit of *Calypso*, so would his ultimate chances of success increase. He might be more apprehensive of

269

Hubbard and the *Lively Lady*, but his initial survey of conditions would have convinced him that the lookouts on the *Lady* were sober, too alert to permit of any operation there.

With *Indefatigable*, as with *Calypso*, it was a different story. *Calypso* had been virtually deserted, easy to take. *Indefatigable* was crowded with the crews of both, but they had been boisterous, far gone in drink, without a thought for possible peril.

Sir Harry, having discovered what Denny Poynter had been about, was almost speechless when Hubbard hailed from alongside.

"It's our steerage," he finally managed. "The cable's apparently been cut, sawed through. We've no rudder."

Hubbard had guessed as much. A skilled diver, with a hack saw, put over the side from a small boat, unnoticed in the gloom, had succeeded in a fairly simple operation. But at such a moment its results were devastating. Sir Harry and his dismayed fellow-captain were forced to the realization that repairs would be far more complicated and time-consuming. Even skilled ship-carpenters and divers, working under such handicaps, could not have the *Indefatigable* under control again for a matter of hours.

Sunlight came in a blinding burst, driving the last vestiges of darkness before it. Light to reveal the plight and distress of the *Indefatigable* even more pitilessly.

Despite the efforts of the officers, only a handful of crewmen were reporting for duty, glassy-eyed, in poor condition to respond to instant orders. Most would have to be left to sleep it off.

Hubbard considered. These were the enemy, and the loss of *Calypso* would be as damaging in the hands of Denny Poynter, perhaps more so, than if she were sent to the bottom by the guns of the *Lively Lady*.

Opposed to that was a sympathy which he could not quite smother for fellow-officers, rivals and enemies though they were, brought low through no real fault of their own. Also, *Calypso*, under an unfamiliar crew but worked by men who were undoubtedly trained seamen and a picked crew, could prove formidable as an adversary for the *Lady* alone. She might well evade them, or – worse – emerge victorious from such an encounter.

Above all, there was Denny Poynter, alive, always dangerous, an implacable enemy. If *Calypso* was to be retaken, it would probably be necessary to board, with an overwhelming force.

"Come aboard, with as many men as are in condition to fight," Hubbard invited. "We'll continue a joint effort, since we all have reason enough."

THIRTY-THREE

"There she is, sir – *Calypso*, right enough."

The lookout's hail was no surprise, once they were out from the harbor. *Calypso* was hull down, propelled by a favoring wind. But the same wind filled every stitch of canvas which Hubbard had been able to crowd on the *Lively Lady*, and the fact that *Calypso* was still in sight was encouraging. Daring and with considerable initiative as he was, Denny Poynter was an indifferent seaman. New to the ship he so suddenly commanded, with a crew equally strange, it would be unusual if they were able to handle their vessel to attain the full measure of speed of which she was capable. That came from knowledge and experience.

He had proffered Sir Harry and Vane-Templeton the courtesy of his quarter-deck, and, though with reddening faces, both had been as quick to accept as to take advantage

272

of his earlier suggestion that they join in the chase – aboard what to them was the *Red Savage*. Nearly a hundred of their combined crew had been awake and sufficiently sober to make the transfer. They would be in condition for battle if called upon to board.

The Marquis, with manifest regret, had returned ashore. As a neutral he could hardly participate in such a chase, however much he might wish.

The British officers had looked about with manifest curiosity, upon finding themselves on an American ship of war. It was as unusual as for Hubbard when he had set foot on Sir Harry's big seventy-four. They could not but be impressed by the discipline and seamanship of these Yankee sailors, Hubbard reflected.

Vane-Templeton broke a long silence.

"We're gaining. They don't properly know how to handle her. Not that they're doing badly, under the circumstances," he added grudgingly.

"We'll have you aboard her, with your own crew, before the day is out," Hubbard promised.

Both captains eyed him curiously, but their attitude had altered from distrust to respect. Another hail came from the lookout.

"She's changing course!"

Calypso was making a short turn, so that for a moment it looked as if, aware that he would be forced to fight, Denny Poynter was anxious to settle the issue without delay. With a man so impulsive, that might be the case, but Hubbard doubted it. Poynter had something in mind.

The tack he was taking would bring them close, but not necessarily within gun range. Then, using the glass, Hubbard understood.

"There's another sail, just showing," he observed, and passed the glass to Sir Harry. "My guess is that it's another pirate – and he had been expecting him."

That was a reasonable assumption. Poynter, learning of three ships immobilized at Fort-de-France, might have sent word to another captain, outlining the excellent possibilities, and this was the response."

"We'll meet him half-way, Mr. Sullivan," Hubbard instructed, and the *Lively Lady* tore over the water as with a matching eagerness. Again, Poynter's impulsiveness had led him to miscalculate. He had planned a joint attack along with the other vessel, but the speed of the *Lady* would insure what he had been at pains to avoid – that the contest would be between the two of them, before the third could come close enough to make a difference.

That the other captain was a judge both of distance and sailing abilities, became apparent as he veered, scuttling for safety like a hen at sight of a hawk. The prospect of coming up to be faced by two enemies, rather than combining for a double attack upon the *Lively Lady*, had alarmed him.

Sir Harry grunted. "He's showing sense!"

Poynter, disconcerted, clearly alarmed at the desertion, was trying, too late, to avoid an unwelcome engagement. Surveying Hubbard's set jaw, the calm with which he gave his orders, Sir Harry could understand Poynter's dismay. Battles were won or lost, in essence, not by ships or guns, but by men.

Only as it became clear that to avoid a fight was out of the question did Poynter turn to meet the inevitable. It was the courage of desperation, and tardy. By the time he could again come around and bring his guns to bear, the *Lively Lady* was plunging down upon him, Hubbard holding his fire. Vane-Templeton grunted approval. It was Hubbard's intention to come alongside, to grapple and board, avoiding as much damage to *Calypso* as possible.

Given their excess of manpower, that would probably succeed, but it required as steady a nerve as hand, and chance was always a factor.

That came in a single wild shot from *Calypso*, also certainly a panicky discharge, but luck directed it. The *Lady's* proud new foremast splintered and came crashing ruinously. For an instant the *Lively Lady* yawed, staggered. Long enough for *Calypso* to unloose her broadside at point-blank range.

This time the error was probably Poynter's; another moment for proper aim might have turned the tide of battle. As it was, the volley ranged high, sweeping the decks, yet with relatively little damage. But there was a scatter of death and destruction, and Hubbard had a sensation as though a giant hand was catching him and flinging him to the deck. He sprawled, senseless.

When he struggled back to consciousness his head and shoulders were soaked and dripping. He stared at a sailor, holding an empty bucket, then, struggling to an elbow, found the ship's doctor on one side, Sir Harry opposite.

Mont Pelee's bald crown swam into his vision as the *Lively Lady* came slowly around. He beheld a shamble of tangled sail and splintered spars, while ugly stains disfigured the decking which Mr. Sullivan had been at pains to keep spotless. Men were furiously at work, restoring order.

"What happened?" he asked, and was as

annoyed as bewildered to find his speech slurred, the words coming from bruised and swollen lips.

"You were struck by flying wreckage," the doctor explained, looking relieved. "Knocked cold for a while – but fortunately it seems not too serious."

Save for a sense of nausea, an awareness of aches and bruises, Hubbard was ready to agree. Matters could easily have been worse. He accepted a hand to regain his feet.

"If you'll excuse me, sir, there are other wounded." The physician was gone. Hubbard stared about, orienting himself. *Calypso* trailed, some distance behind, but the Union Jack was back in place, steady in the breeze. At this distance she showed no sign of damage.

"You retook her? And Captain Vane-Templeton's back aboard?"

Sir Harry was actually smiling.

"And manned, sufficiently for the moment, by her proper crew," he confirmed. "Your maneuver put us alongside within moments after your accident, and Vane-Templeton led the boarders, spearheaded by your crew," he added. "It was scarcely a fight."

Their position was approximately what it had been a couple of days before, when the

277

Marquis had intervened between them. They were back in neutral waters.

In sudden puzzlement increasing to anxiety he looked about for his own officers – Sullivan, Sandys, even Richter. With himself incapacitated, some of them should have been on the quarter-deck.

"That broadside was badly aimed, yet destructive," Dupont explained. "The doctor tells me you lost a dozen men killed, as many more injured. Among the latter are Misters Sullivan and Richter. Mr. Sandys was killed outright."

But indeed. His lieutenants incapacitated along with himself, at the moment when the ship was most in need of proper handling. Victory had been within Denny Poynter's grasp –

Meeting his eyes, Sir Harry colored uncomfortably.

"I trust you will overlook what under normal circumstances would have been an unwarrantable liberty on my part," he explained. "But with no one else able to do so, I assumed temporary command. Your crew afforded me every cooperation."

Hubbard eyed him wonderingly, then with a warmer sense of friendliness. However ironical, this was a crowning touch to the oddly assorted series of events, a full return of favors. Beyond doubt, that action on Sir Harry's part had preserved victory, prevented defeat. That the taking or sinking of the *Lively Lady* would have been as disastrous for the British on board her as for herself, would with Sir Harry have been a secondary consideration.

"The lion and the lamb," Hubbard murmured, and held out his hand. Sir Harry goggled a moment, then, understanding, returned the clasp.

"Oh, er – precisely," he agreed, and again his face lightened. "Though if I represent the proverbial British lion, the matching simile is less than accurate. There's nothing lamb-like about you when it comes to battle, Hubbard."

"It's a damned shame that this war may set us to fight each other again," Hubbard returned. For the moment they were speaking their minds, men who respected each other, with a growing liking. "I – now what's this?"

Dupont was staring with equal surprise and outrage at a newcomer, a converted merchantman by her looks. She came under full sail, cutting out suddenly from the shelter of the headland, plunging with a reckless abandon between the *Calypso* and the *Lady*. The colors of England stood straight in the breeze.

"It's peace!" A tall figure shouted as the

other ship tore past. "The war's over. Peace between England and the United States! I'll return with the details –"

His words were lost in the wind, as he kept on to take the word to a possibly hostile *Calypso*. Peace! It was the fact which mattered. Details were unimportant. Hubbard and Sir Harry stared after him, then, meeting each other's eyes, clasped hands anew.

THIRTY-FOUR

"Our problem seems to have resolved itself," Sir Harry was in meditative mood. "I mean, as to when or how we shall depart. All our differences blown away!"

"All, Sir Harry?"

"All," Captain Dupont returned firmly. "If you're thinking of the Lady Renee – as I know damned well you are, and no wonder – then keep right on, with my blessing. Upon acquaintance I find her charming and wonderful. You know, the *Lively Lady* might well have been named in her honor. But it was all a mistake, that notion of an alliance between she and myself. And I've known for some time that it was not at all to her liking. She's had eyes and heart only for you."

He stared across the bay to the *Indefatigable*, beyond to the beach and the city against the backdrop of greenery.

"As for myself, the same sentiments have come to apply, since I've had the privilege of making the acquaintance of Miss O'Hara. And that's another debt I owe you, Hubbard. She has told me of the service you rendered her brother and herself."

Hubbard was hardly surprised. From the outset it had been plain that there was a mutual attraction.

"I trust that congratulations are in order?"

Sir Harry reddened boyishly.

"I believe they will be. I intend to make sure that they are, at the very first opportunity. And – begad, there's a welcoming party at the quay – the Governor, of course – and Constance – arm in arm with Renee – she's waving to you! Begad, the Lively Lady –"

Sighting Hubbard's wave in return, Renee was executing a lively jig-step on the sand. Constance swung to join her.

For a third time, very solemnly, Hubbard and Sir Harry shook hands.

"After the way you've fought both us and the pirates, Captain Hubbard – magnificent actions, I might add – it would appear that there should be no further difficulties for you or your crew. No lingering taint of treason or piracy, such as Poynter sought to fix upon you. But in the unlikely event that the question should ever arise, I'll be only too happy, along with Vane-Templeton, to testify that it's a tissue of lies."